TALI

On that haunted, experimental planet there must still hide an inhuman questing intelligence. In the derelict Frames of Talisker, the Alien that had supplied the Gene-key still lingered.

A screen glowed, starlight blazed, Talisker loomed, and Liz had the sensation of Phase, with the brain's electronic messages slightly out of key with the skull, so that she seemed to be in a hundred contingent fields of space-time at once; they cleared and she could see Talisker as it had appeared to Spingarn.

Blazing, sun-drenched ice-caps towered and splintered. Roads—roads? Or rather energy bands curled and vanished into chasms where vast humanoids stood about in dumb malice; engines roared across violet skies, and always there was a random progress of events, tortuous, eerie, spasmodic . . .

What new personality could even the robotic Guardians create that could successfully maintain equilibrium where an Alien Frame-maker stalked the planet?

Planet Probability

by

BRIAN N. BALL

DAW BOOKS, INC.
DONALD A. WOLLHEIM, PUBLISHER

1301 Avenue of the Americas
New York, N. Y. 10019

COVER ART BY KELLY FREAS.

DEDICATION:

In memory of
E. J. Carnell

First Printing: January 1973

PRINTED IN U.S.A.

Planet Probability

CHAPTER

★ 1 ★

There were the two fliers, midgets in the gray sky of over three hundred thousand dawns ago. They had circled that empty sky, just as they did now in this fragment of film. Liz Hassell was conscious of an aching sense of wonder; the past had truly happened, its ghosts still lingered. And they haunted her. The set assistant, a high-grade robot, asked whether it should run the bit of film again. Marvell shook his head.

"I believe," he said to Liz Hassell and the other young trainee, Dyson, "in an approximation of reality." He rested his bulk on the side of the staging-bubble and looked down into the dark arena where something like a hundred thousand men and a few women were waiting, unconscious and in the final stages of memory-recycling, to try his latest re-creation. He was worried. "We haven't all the data. So we must approximate. What do you think?"

He was dressed in what he considered to be the appropriate garments for the period—not unlike those of the Savior of Civilization, thought Liz Hassell. He had the black frock coat, the narrow striped trousers, the white leather spats and the gay cravat of the Mechanical Age impresario who had come to the rescue of mankind just about the time of the Disinvention of Work. The clothes emphasized Marvell's bulk. Liz disliked heavy men. She turned to her fellow trainee who was a slim handsome bisexual she had once adored; now Dyson was nothing to her. His overwhelming charm, his instant enthusiasm, his boyish mannerisms, grated on her; she saw them as a kind of witless affectation. Predictably, Dyson said:

"It's going to be terrific, Marvell! It's going to have them lining up in queues all the way to the end of the Galaxy! They've never seen anything like it! What a Plot! And the casualty rate! Thirty percent in the first few hours?"

"Something like that," said Marvell.

"Well! Ideal for all the certified psychopaths! Isn't that what we're short of, a suicidal Plot that doesn't strain credibility?"

Marvell frowned. He thought Dyson, top student in his training year, unimpressive. About Liz Hassell his feelings were mixed. She had the trick of finding material that others could not imagine existed; and she could set up a Possibility Curve with the best of them; but she lacked a certain panache. She wanted things wrapped up neatly, too neatly. He looked at her slim, rounded figure; the black hair was natural, the eyes too of ordinary human pigmentation; she was neither tall nor short, beautiful nor common. Neat. Ordinary, unaffected, competent. He wasn't too sure that he wanted to hear what she'd have to say.

"Run the early sequences," he told the languid robot, whose flat gray carapace had all the signs of robotic boredom. "The Terran film!" snarled Marvell, as the automaton delayed.

Liz Hassell saw that his heavy black moustaches were wet where he had chewed them; he was sweating beneath the tall black hat. He had fallen in love with the Mechanical Age, and he had adopted its dress, customs and mannerisms. Well, each to his soul-place, she thought. She herself had never quite got over a yearning for a more primitive era, though she kept the inclination to herself. Short-stay trips in the Frames were one thing, but should Comp get the idea that you were psychologically in tune with a period that had a number of vacancies—as with the Sub-Men Frames—they might yank you out of Direction altogether. What with the really frightful carnivores, and competition from other bipeds, Java Man had a thin and dangerous time of it. Most of the permanent inhabitants of the Third Sub-Man Frame were Time-outers. Liz grinned. There'd be a few calling Time-out when the Plot below began to roll. Her face became serious as the ancient recording she had found was shown.

"Exquisite!" murmured Dyson, allowing his long blond hair to swish from side to side.

"It's good," admitted Marvell. He adjusted the purple and yellow cravat at his throat. "How it survived I'll never know—Liz, here it comes!"

The robot had adjusted a small total-experience simulator which could translate the ancient piece of film into an approximation of three-dimensional life. The scene was blurred, vague, unstable; but the figures in the white fog were human beings. As yet, they were unrecognizable individually. The amateur cameraman who had probably died in this war of antiquity had not mastered his recording machine. But it was *real*! Liz shuddered. How had this fragment of celluloid escaped the holocausts of the Mad Wars? This, together with a few charred remnants of books and the odd medallion or piece of statuary, was all that remained of the era. It was as though the Terrans of the Nuclear Ages had wished to erase the origins of their civilization. She had found the film in a vault on one of the planets of Andromeda ZU 58, though what archaeologist had deposited it was unknown; the obsolete and melancholy custodian of the museum thought the film had lain there for over half a millennium. And no, it knew of no more such caches, though it realized how valuable they were.

The film jumped into focus at last, and there was a misted dawn over a flat landscape with broken trees splintered by violent explosions. The foreground was still shadowy, yet the blurred and unstable figures were real men, youngsters with long rifles and fixed bayonets; on their heads, rakishly, mushroom-shaped helmets, and cigarettes drooping from their mouths. Liz savored the smoke. The totex machines gave you the stench of the battlefield, its rum and coffee, the cigarettes, a hint of corruption from the green long-dead. She saw the better shots now. One man smiling dreamily at a memory: he was the one who was catapulted back, shot at the moment of the advance; the angular-jawed young captain beside him took a sip of coffee. And Liz experienced a helpless sense of belonging—a kind of angry pity that was part-identification; and then the officer, a cheerfully handsome man, smiled confidently into the camera lens. A wry grin at the slippery mud of the trench. Marvell's voice came as if from a thousand miles away.

"The simply incredible thing about it is that there were people, they lived, they spoke, they acted as we see them now. And anyone can have it all! All of it!"

He had touched a chord in the girl's imagination for a moment, but the sight of his broad, fleshy face and its sweat brought her back to the present; Marvell overdid his effects. No wonder he sweated and chewed the black moustaches! The fliers he'd put into the Plot were too much.

The stench of fetid water hit Liz as the totex showed a glimpse of the soldiers' feet; they were up to their ankles in watery mud; one dropped a cigarette and cursed silently. They were desperately keyed up now. Liz thought suddenly that this was why she was in Direction rather than tramping contentedly through green savannahs behind some huge-jawed mate from the dawn of humanity; for her it was more important to make the Frames than to live in them.

"It's a lovely bit of war, Liz," said Marvell. "Lovely, uncomplicated rituals. See, they're ready!"

And they were. About two score of young men, some with only minutes of life before them; one would soon topple back toward the unidentified cameraman, ending the brief glimpse into trench warfare of the Mechanical Age.

"He's raising his whistle!" Dyson squealed. "Oh, see!"

The young officer was serious. Comp had explained the purpose of the whistle: part symbolic, part functional. It had talismanic qualities, for it brought the fliers into the combat.

"There they go!" Marvel exclaimed.

A silent sustained blast, the men scrambling over the top of the slippery trench wall, and a boy of twenty hurtling back toward the camera; and that was all, except for the few seconds of mysterious film that showed the fliers. It wasn't much of a record for Comp to build a whole Plot on.

The robot beside the totex globe waited until the last ancient flickering moments of blackness had ceased.

"Sir?" it addressed Marvell. "Run the flying machines in greater depth?"

Marvell frowned, for the robot had guessed his anxiety. Dyson told it to go ahead, but Marvell's pride would not allow the showing.

"Leave it," he said. "Cigar!" he yelled to a servo-robot which skittered across on spidery legs with a fat cigar glowing. It had waited an hour for this moment; when Marvell took the cigar, it was a sign that the memory-cassettes had almost completed their work in the skulls below. Individual memory-cells were biting deeper and deeper into the subconscious minds of the thousands who had opted for the experimental Plot; tiny clusters of cells would be smashing through nerve-tissue in the quiet and receptive bodies, racing with bewildering speed through the vital areas of control to restructure the psyche so that it could cope with the demands of the Plot. Information roared in a colossal stream into the deep, submerged areas, planting colonies of memory, detailing the background each man and woman could expect to have acquired, modifying a million million corners of hints of recollection, and gnawing with a monstrous power at all that had occurred in their minds!

Liz could see some of the gently respiring figures when she used her scanner; it amazed her that each one was being imbued with a new persona. But could the restructured minds cope with the Plot? Was it viable?

Any new Plot could go wrong, which was why Comp had to recheck and doublecheck against the possibility that humans couldn't adapt to the new circumstances with which they were faced. Liz shrugged. Comp said *go,* and that was enough for Marvell.

There would be a re-creation of the ritual warfare of the Mechanical Age. Real mud, real rifles, real death. And real flying traction-engines.

Somehow Marvell had convinced Comp that the Possibility Space of the Mechanical Age had room for his beloved steam engines. Not only that, but that they were tied up with the fetish he was hung up on, that of Mechanical Man's absorption with personal conveyances. A statistical test of significance had shown that he might be right. Liz Hassell shrugged again beneath the elegant fur she wore. He could be right. But if he wasn't, there'd be thousands yelling to get out of the Plot in a short time; and what was to happen to the delicate balance of the Frames if a sudden demand for Time-out on this scale should occur? After all, only suicidal maniacs wanted to be in a Plot like this one of Marvell's; they looked for quick death, most of them, but not in an idiot world, not in one the human mind couldn't accept as possible! Where could they be placed at short notice if the Plot failed?

No wonder Marvell was worried!

"I had a look at the fliers in the old film," Dyson was saying to an uninterested Marvell. "Yesterday I checked it with Comp. They'd got the speed to that of the fliers—about ninety miles an hour. Agrees beautifully with the technology of the age! And the overall weight allowed quite a lot of projectile power. Why, they'd managed to absorb all the recoil from the howitzer without going out of the technological possibilities!"

Liz saw Marvell's indecision. She felt unaccustomedly bitchy.

"I looked in on Comp too," she said. "They said Spingarn didn't like the steam—"

"Spingarn!" Marvell bawled, face red. "Never say Spingarn! It's bad luck!"

Dyson hadn't learned to curb his impulsiveness. He chattered intelligently:

"Wasn't that the Plot Director whose persona went aberrant—the thing about random vari—"

"Shut up!" roared Marvell, stabbing his cigar squarely onto the gray carapace of the set-robot. It allowed itself a high-pitched whine of protest. "I never want to hear that name again! Never! It's not just bad luck—it's lunacy! Liz, don't do it again!" He kicked the machine for protesting.

Dyson sulked. His troubles were just beginning, thought Liz Hassell. He'd never make Plot Director, however much he enthused. He'd be back in the Frames before long. The thought was some consolation to her, for she had suffered a month of cold hell on Cygnus VIII not long ago, when he had told her their affair was over. It was taking too much of his organic energy, he told her. His career was suffering. There had been a ferocious mutant struggle going on at the time in the Cygnus Frame: Liz had found herself recycled amongst long-headed things with wet skin and webbed feet. It had been the only opening at short notice for a nubile young woman of her dimensions. She shuddered at the memory. Dyson would pay. When he was dismissed from Direction, she would see that he was dropped off into a Geriatric Frame for virgin spinsters. And keep him there.

"Starting time?" Marvell snapped at the robot he had offended.

"Three minutes, sir," it said, still hurt. "May I take this opportunity of wishing you a great success?"

There was metallic irony in its voice. Marvell took a second cigar from the eager servo and blew smoke over the high-grade's lizard-metal gray skin; it wrinkled at the pollution. Marvell blew again. It didn't protest. With Marvell, neither men nor machines raised too much fuss; he wasn't one of the hotshot Directors, and it was rumored that he'd lost the confidence of the Director of the Frames. But he was still Marvell, Liz's boss. To her surprise, Marvell insisted she give her opinion of the new venture.

"You've worked on it for months, Liz—is it a goer? I mean, I know you've reservations."

She smiled at him. When he spoke in this unconfident manner she found him almost appealing; if only he hadn't so much sheer bulk! He could do with restructuring. She answered him carefully, to help his distrust of his work.

"I saw the reruns of some of the bits you tried—I liked them all, Marvell. But I think Comp's put you way out on a limb with this linkup between personal transportation and ritual war. See!" she said suddenly, snapping her fingers at the sulking robot. "Close focus on the fliers. Quick!"

"Only two minutes before we start," Dyson said. "Shouldn't we be getting clear of the area? There's going to be a lot of projectiles whizzing about soon, and the staging-bubbles won't stand up to them."

Marvell and Liz ignored him as the totex globe unwound snakily and the tiny fragment of recorded history flickered like the shadow of a ghost across the screens. It chilled Liz Hassell to see it. A few seconds of dim images preserved by some blind chance: the only record that was anything like coherent of the flying machines of the Mechanical Age. And there they were, two blurred gray shapes half a mile above the trench where the young officer and his men waited for death; the cameraman had swung his lens up, or perhaps had the camera torn from his hands. But the pictures existed. Two vague machines, size unknown, but unquestionably man-made. Altogether the wrong dimensions for animals or birds; and with a lazy deadliness about the way they circled like fragile predators above the battlefield. Comp thought they were engaged in some kind of ritual exchange of courtesies before swooping down to join the muddy and desperate encounters below. And maybe Comp was right.

"It could be viable, couldn't it, Liz?" Marvell asked.

"Of course!" Dyson gushed.

"One minute before commencement," reported the set-robot. "You should move away for your own safety, sir."

"I liked part of it," Liz said, ignoring the interruptions. "I loved the close combat sequences—they'll have nothing to complain about there. The casualty list's going to be as high as that of the Solar Drift cultists, and they burn up at quite a rate. I liked the mud and the diseases. Comp could be entirely right about that side of things. But I have this creepy sensation that they're wrong in deriving a correspondence between your steam engines and the fliers we saw just now."

"Please clear the area!" implored the robot, forgetting its hurt feelings.

Comp added a warning. A suave voice echoed over the immense Plotting hall:

"Director Marvell! Your Plot goes forward in thirty seconds! All personnel are advised to enter protected areas immediately. Otherwise, they must be removed by Security operatives."

Marvell threw his second cigar away. It would be undignified to be hauled away by some cheerfully tender Security robot. He jumped into the staging-bubble and made room for Liz. Dyson stared openmouthed as Marvell punched buttons. He was still standing, amazed and dismayed, as they were swept away.

"Spingarn!" growled Marvell at Liz Hassell. "He said the same thing."

The staging-bubble skittered for the safe areas at a tremendous pace. Liz Hassell felt excited, nervous, almost fearful; every time the name of Spingarn came up, Marvell lost all his authority. It meant something vital to him;

she could see it in his eyes. He looked like a bewildered stallion, all his strength and power of no use. *Spingarn . . .* why?

"I know. Comp said Spingarn was against the traction-engines."

"Then how the hell did they get their fliers into the air? They'd no nuclear power—that came later! There's no trace of electrical motive power on Terra! It has to be steam!"

"I expect you're right," she said quietly, and the answer calmed him. She didn't care now about the rightness or wrongness of Comp's guesses. The thrill of Plotting had her in its grip. She could almost feel the huge slow entering into consciousness of the thousands of combatants below. They would have new memories. Speech patterns; voice rhythms; recognition signals; endless personality data. Enough political knowledge to make some sense of the war they fought in—enough for barely-educated peasants! And the skills to handle the cumbersome and deadly weapons they carried. For the officers, a sufficient grasp of tactics to keep them alive in the strange wet and broken plain. What a vast concourse of ideas subliminally battered into the minds of these twenty-ninth century men to make them into warriors of antiquity! Liz looked ahead. As the bubble reached the protected areas of the hall, powerful scanners reared up.

She could zoom in on any part of the colossal battlefield, where it was now past dawn and the white mist was forming in eerie hanging pockets over the broken trees and the trembling soldiery of a long-forgotten war. Marvell's hangups didn't matter; nor did Comp's cold assessments. The re-creation over which she had labored for so long had taken shape—was *beginning*! And all those men down below who had chosen the roaring life—however short!—of the Frames in preference to their own feeble attempts to fill an oversufficiency of leisure were taking part in *her* Plot!

"Director Marvell's new Mechanical Age Ritual Combat Plot!" intoned Comp. "Ten seconds!"

Marvell dismissed the staging-bubble with a sweep of his hand. He was interested in the skies. Neither he nor Liz saw a scurrying servo-robot, blank-faced and impersonal, bearing down on them with its brain-globe shining importantly. It began throwing out unskillful mind-alerts as it drew to a halt, and Marvell caught the full impact. Liz's eyes were on the trench where faces flowered into shocked awareness of danger, and hands gripped the damp wooden stocks of rifles.

"Director Marvell!" the servo bellowed. Its beamers again struck at Marvell, who turned, staggered and yelled back:

"Cut them!"

It was not to be thwarted.

"Director Marvell! Immediately! By the Director of the Frames—now, at once! Marvell to come!"

"Now!" Comp intoned.

"No!" Marvell roared.

"My God," Liz said as *Götterdämmerung* began.

The snouts of huge cannon breathed unholy life into the Plot and men began to die. Above, in the wide gray sky of early morning, tiny glittering specks appeared. Whistles were raised to mouths by freshly shaved young officers.

"The Director said now!" bawled the servo-robot, beamers turned off. "Now, sir!"

Dyson was flung into the protected area by a guffawing Security robot; it unwound its tentacles from his shaking, furious body with tender concern.

"What's happening?" squealed Dyson. "You left me—"

Marvell grinned at Liz.

"Tell him," he said. "Enjoy the Plot—our master needs me!" He climbed into the staging-bubble which had been directed to the protected area by the efficient, languid set-robot.

"And the young lady!" bawled the servo above the roar of battle and Dyson's questions.

Liz had turned back, fascinated, to see the fliers approaching, their smokestacks blasting out a whirling shower of sparks and thick black smoke; the pilots were yelling with delight at the feeling of power as wings flapped noisily and engineers threw fuel into open grates. Already one machine was aligning its howitzer. *And it was all wrong!* Liz was about to voice her sureness when she felt herself pulled away; off-balance, she would have fallen had not the Security robot flicked a network of whippy tentacles to steady her and place her beside Marvell.

"Me!" she gasped, understanding coming slowly. "Not me!"

"You!" Marvell growled.

"Why?"

The servo raced beside the fast bubble.

"I know!" it shouted. "I got additional instructions on the way here, miss! Comp advised the Director that you'd be useful too!"

"For what?" snarled Marvell, glaring ahead as they raced through the long corridors toward the heart of the most sophisticated piece of hardware the human race had built. "Why does the Director want *me*?"

Liz began to dislike Marvell again.

"Oh, yes! I know!" the servo boasted.

"Tell me!"

"The Director said I should, sir! And Miss Hassell! It's Spingarn, sir!"

"Spingarn!"

Liz Hassell heard the note of baffled fear.

"I said Spingarn was bad luck! You shouldn't have mentioned him, you crazy bitch! If this is something to do with your turning up data on the—"

"It's Spingarn on Talisker!" the servo called, anxious to pass on the information. "Talisker, sir! You know—where Spingarn went!"

Liz Hassell's brilliant orange-flecked green eyes shone with a dangerous fire: she had been so keyed up over the Plot, so full of a tender and ghostly pity for the men of three hundred thousand dawns ago, so amazed that something she had had a hand in creating was to begin, that she could barely absorb this new turn of events. *Crazy bitch!* Marvell had called her. The arrogant bastard! She turned to tell him what she thought of him when she saw his staring eyes, his haunted face and the terrible fears in it. He wasn't looking at her at all.

Marvell whispered something. She just caught the words:

"I know Talisker. *Another name for Hell!*"

CHAPTER

★ 2 ★

LIVE! roared the mind-searing beamers outside the office of the Director of Frames. Marvell shouted to the humanoid secretary to tone them down to a level through which conversation could be heard. It waved negligently at the battery of tiny spheres clustered around the great bronze doors; they jangled into silence for a moment, and the subtle shifting hypnotic patterns of sensory impressions were stilled. A kind of peace settled on them, but only for a few seconds. It was their duty to spread the message of the Frames: nothing could halt them.

"Jesus!" growled Marvell, tilting his black hat back to show a gleaming and sweat-covered bald head. "I have to wait? After speeding here like a maniac?"

"I'm afraid so, sir," the humanoid said. It smiled a green fluorescent smile equally at Liz and Marvell. "The Director is in conference with the Head of Disaster Control."

The beamers began again. *Live in new dimensions!* insidiously squeaked one, conjuring up in Liz's mind an entire sequence of gossamer-winged creatures swarming toward the Crab Nebula; young, most of them, with faces like angels. And no wonder, thought Liz Hassell, for they were almost paralyzed with drugs. *Ride with us!* another beamer insisted, taking her abruptly for a few white-hot seconds into a searing desert on one of the Artificial Worlds of the Seventh Asiatic Confederation: and she was astride a wild gray mare, hair like a black sail in the wind and ahead one of the Confederation's silver yoni-towers!

She fought free of the mind-blasting impact, to try to hear what Marvell was saying for the second or third time:

"Why you, Liz?"

But the beamers had got to her now, and they would not let go. *BE THERE!* one demanded, and this one could find an echo of sympathy, so that it projected instantly the Sub-Man Frame she liked. There was the volcano, the ground-trembler! Worshiped by shambling men who had once walked on Earth, it sent a plume of fire into the blue sky. Liz Hassell wished herself two million years away from the coming encounter with the Director of Frames. *Be a savage! Hunt the red apes!* and Liz's heart sang *yes!*

"Turn them down!" Marvell growled, and again the glowing secretary waved a hand, bringing peace.

"Liz! Don't let them get to you!" Marvell said. And the beamers chimed again, for theirs was a sacred trust.

"All right!" Liz cried.

"Give them an edge and they flood you," Marvell said. "Keep them out! Think of Spingarn!"

"Yes!" she cried. "I think that's it—Springarn! It has to be. The servo was on the way to pick you up and Comp remembered that I'd asked about him." And she could keep the insistent clamoring out now, for there was the thrill of the Plot again. "The Director heard us talking—I expect he was having your conversations monitored, and one of the Comp circuits got clever and keyed me in to my request. Easy, Marvell!"

Marvell was still distressed; she did not feel so full of anger now.

"Then why me? What have I done?" he snarled at the humanoid.

It smiled sweetly.

The servo put in eagerly:

"We were to tell you it's Talisker, sir! I expect you've heard—"

The green-faced secretary silenced it with a whiplash of electronic hate. The little servo backed off.

"Well?" snapped Marvell, unimpressed.

"We were just to tell you 'Spingarn.' Spingarn of Talisker," the secretary said blandly. "Nothing else."

"Then why send for me—and why keep me waiting when I've a Plot up for proving?"

"I'm sorry about the delay, sir. The Director had trouble locating the Head of Disaster Control. They're still in together."

"So they're having a conference! Why bring me?"

"Well, sir," the humanoid said, "you should know. You did know Spingarn better than most of us."

"You!" Liz Hassell said. "Spingarn the Probability Man!"*

"It was years ago—"

"Eighteen months," the humanoid put in.

"Before my time in Direction," Liz said to herself.

"So it's only two years!" Marvell growled.

"A year and a half," the secretary insisted. "And no news since the Genekey specification came back."

"Genekey?" Liz said.

"Genekey," repeated Marvell.

Liz waited, but Marvell said nothing. Her mind raced. Comp had been cagey about Spingarn. *Genekey*? There had been rumors about some kind of genetic experiments. . . . *Spingarn?*

"Genes?" she asked Marvell. Apologetically, she went on, "I should know. The Director—"

Marvell faced her. The girl was right. She should not have to go before the mad spider of a man who was the Director of Frames quite unprepared.

"Brandies!" he called to the humanoid. It crossed to a cabinet and poured three large drinks. Liz sipped.

"Well?" she said.

"You'd better be told," he said. "The Genekey stabilized the worst of the random-cell variables. Oh, Jesus!" he growled, seeing the complete incomprehension on her face. "What do you know?"

The beamers began to chime again, but the humanoid did something to discourage them; it wanted to hear all of this. Marvell saw that it was snooping, but he was past caring.

"About what?" Liz asked. "What do I know about what?"

"All this!"

"Random-cell variables?"

"No! Leave that! Something simple for a start! The Frames. Probability. Start there!"

* Read *The Probability Man*—Brian N. Ball, also in Daw Books.

The girl saw that he was serious, seriously trying to help her. She humored him. All his ebullience was gone.

"The Frames are easy. There's nothing for most of mankind to do anymore. Work is over. It's been disinvented. So we have to fill time with Possibility Space. We create happenings."

"You always were lucid," Marvell said. He looked at the slender arms. The girl was dressed in rippling yellow fur; beneath the mottled skin was a suspicion of smooth, full flesh. He had never noticed her before, not as a sex-object. "Probability?"

She smiled.

"We don't know what worlds existed in some eras. There's only vague legend. So we have to build up what we can from the evidence left. We're well-informed about the origins of the human race and everything that happened after the Mad Wars. We do a dilly of a Frame on the Asiatic Confederations, and something to take your breath away on the Sub-Men. But we don't know much about your favorite time."

"And?"

"And if we don't know, we approximate."

"Yes! Those damned fliers!" He turned to the humanoid. It was sipping brandy elegantly. "How's the new Plot going?"

The green-faced automaton shook its fluorescent head. "Can't say yet, sir. Not till it's been checked out by Comp. But there's been no Disaster yet—there hasn't been a call for Time-out either."

Marvell sighed.

"That's something," Liz said. "Dyson will monitor it for us."

"Dyson?" spat Marvell. "Now there's someone who should get to know about Talisker! But go on, Liz."

"Probability?"

"You've covered it."

"I haven't."

"So go on!"

"Comp evaluates historical records and says what probably happened."

"And Spingarn ruined the probabilities! Why couldn't he stick to Plotting? Brilliant stuff he turned in! Why go for random variables?"

"He did that?"

"That's Spingarn!"

"But how?"

"That," the humanoid put in suavely, "if you don't mind my saying so, sir, and you, miss, would take more time than you have at the moment. Will you please enter?"

Marvell hesitated.

"The Director? I mean—the Genekey worked?"

He was recalling with a numb horror what he had seen some eighteen months before when Spingarn had disappeared into the remote and horrific world of Talisker. Then, the Director had still been in the grip of a frightful gene-transmutation that had turned him into a thing from nightmare: a monstrous admixture of man and snake that reared out of radiant yellow mud. Marvell shuddered. He could see again the snake's head, the red wet mouth, the iridescent steely hairs, the skeletal arms that waved about and showered Spingarn and himself with gobbets of stinking detritus. A vast and terrible rage had convulsed it. And it talked! *"Spingarn!"* the thing had breathed, choking with a sick rage. *"Spingarn, who took a fancy to the extremities of the probability function and did a bit of adjusting here and a touch of recycling there and who changed my gene structure when I went to visit Talisker to inspect his experiments! And made me into a thing like this!"*

"Do go in, sir. It really worked. The Director is himself once more." It smiled. "It would be only fair for me to tell you, though: he still has his memories."

Liz Hassell shivered too. She had heard of the mysterious Spingarn's experiments, but this was something new. *What had happened?* And how was she, Liz Hassell, twenty-four years old, a slim and bright girl with a future in Direction, connected with the strange genius Spingarn?

"The Director," insisted the humanoid secretary.

Marvell walked to the great bronze doors like a man in a trance; his wide shoulders were bowed. He looks middle-aged! thought Liz Hassell, who had always considered Marvell a slightly older contemporary. His showman's ebullience had deserted him. The impresario's clothes hung slackly on his defeated figure.

The doors swung open and Liz saw what few underlings had seen, the center of the web that controlled almost all human life. The room was as big as the complete lower deck of an interstellar cruiser, huge, low, stone-floored, and with serried rows of scanners that were both empty and pulsating with latent energy, blue and eager. *So this is it! The center of it all!* She watched Marvell reluctantly face the desk in the center of the enormous room. And Marvell audibly groaned with relief, for the man who sat at the desk was recognizably a man, with a high-domed head, a thin long neck eroded by age, long arms, and black eyes like polished stones. Beside him was a powerful, muscular man, large-headed, dark-skinned, with thick arms hanging slightly forward. She knew him as Deneb, the Head of Disaster Control. Impressive though he was, it was the Director who dominated the scene. Liz gulped as a reedy voice issued from the wet red lips of the most powerful man in the Galaxy.

"How sorry I was to drag you away from your first proving of the new Plot!"

"I—" began Marvell, hat askew, bald head shining with sweat. "I came at once, sir. So Spingarn—" and he let the words hang there.

"Spingarn!" Deneb snapped. "That's why we need you."

"Oh, we need you, Marvell!" the Director fluted. "Who else could we call on?"

Liz saw the strange hatred of the man. Who was it directed against? There was a purring quality in his voice, but underlying it was a howl of anguish. What had Marvell done to arouse such a fury?

"He was just a colleague—"

"More!" the old voice insisted hatefully. "You were Spingarn's confidant—his friend—his adviser even."

"No! Never! I warned him—"

"Why so modest, Marvell? You, the man who encouraged him with his random probability research!"

There was something grotesque about Marvell's fear. Such a large man so bitterly afraid! And Liz was infected with his terrors. She moved quietly behind him, interposing his bulk between herself and the source of danger. It was a pattern of behavior that would have made Liz laugh only minutes before; she did not despise herself, though. The hatred was real, and the evil she saw in the Director's stone-like eyes was real.

"Who else?" the man muttered.

"Not me, sir!" Marvell said hastily. "Encourage

Spingarn! Never! The man was a lunatic—he should have been kept in the Gunpowder Frame! He's no more than a wrecker, sir—why, I knew nothing about the reactivation of Talisker—nothing, sir, nothing!"

The old man giggled.

"Oh, Marvell! You know, Miss Hassell, your immediate superior has this delightful ability to see fun in everything! How happy you'll be together! You, dear, with your meticulous scholarship, and our own Marvell with his panache and blundering recklessness!" The black eyes were full of a sudden rage that sent shivers down the girl's spine once more; the old man was a powerful and evil thing, quite outside her range of experience. "You wondered, Miss Hassell," he said, "why I asked for you?"

"I did."

She answered in a firm enough voice, but she felt completely lost. What did the stone eyes see? Why did he hate? What did he want?

"My dear," sneered the hateful, insidious voice, and she knew he hated her youth, her energy. "Why? A whim! An old man's fancy!"

"No," she whispered, certain. "It wasn't."

"So it wasn't! How right the young lady can be! Eh, Marvell? Eh, Deneb?"

"Comp was right," Deneb agreed. "It mostly is right on probability."

"Not always!" snarled the Director. "But this time, yes! You see, my dear," he said, turning back to Liz, "you brought it on yourself! I sent for Marvell because he was the one associate of Spingarn's that might be able to cope with Talisker—"

"Not Talisker!" groaned Marvell. "Not me!"

"You!" the Director said harshly. "Why not? And you too, Miss Hassell, for your curiosity. I asked for anything that might impinge on Spingarn and Talisker, and Comp remembered at last that you'd been curious about Spingarn. You've been too inquisitive, Miss Hassell!"

Liz quailed. Whatever was terrifying Marvell, this senile old man's hatred was worse.

The Head of Disaster Control tried to apologize. Reasonably, he said:

"If we could have sent our regular operatives in, we would have done so, miss. But they're conditioned to eventualities that can take place. I mean, give them a Byzantine palace revolution that goes wrong, and they'll go in with a knife or a spear or a well-designed bit of rabble-rousing and eliminate the trouble. They'll even take over one of Marvell's crazy fliers, six-inch howitzers and all, if they're detailed. They're trained! And good! Ask them to clean up a mess in a regular Plot, and they'll do it. But what could anyone with a normal mind make of Talisker? And you did ask for Spingarn!"

"Oh dear!" the Director giggled hatefully. "Oh dear me! You don't even know what Talisker is!"

"She does," Marvell said in a hollow voice. "She's a bright girl. Too damned bright! She said the fliers were crazy from the first."

The Director's cold eyes turned again to the girl. There was no word for Marvell, and no more mock amusement. "Talisker?"

"Yes," said Liz Hassell, remembering with a fearful clarity what she had found in the recesses of one of the old memory-banks that no one troubled to use anymore now that Comp knew everything and was ready to oblige. "It was where the Frames began. They had to start somewhere. And in secret."

Talisker!

A planet chosen for its remoteness. And it had to be remote, so that the secret of the new kind of human experience should not leak out too soon. It had to be secret, this ultimate development that could manufacture a complete new persona, a new self, for those bored to almost suicidal depression with the sameness, the safety, the security of modern life. But Talisker was hundreds of years old! It was a ruin, an abandoned museum!

Empty and eerie, full of ghosts and the echoes of past ringing Plots, it held only residual memories and ancient triumphs! Only the wreckage of a hundred experimental Frames served to mark the passage of man. It was a planetary museum, a mausoleum, nothing but a barren world! As Liz told it in her economical, measured voice, she was haunted by the sense of the past once more. And she was deathly afraid of what the evil old man would say.

"Excellent!" he murmured. "A credit to our selection procedures!"

"Don't involve me in Talisker!" Marvell burst out. "I don't want to—"

"Quiet!" the old man said viciously. "Marvell, there's not the time for your imbecilic remarks! Look!"

He passed a skilled hand over the sensor-pads on his desk; they wavered toward him, eager to absorb instructions from his blue-veined stong hands; and the low, vast room was flooded with images of the lonely planet far out on the rim of the Galaxy, the lost planet of Talisker!

"You are there!" sneered the old man. *"Live in one of a thousand worlds!"*

The words burned into Liz Hassell's mind. They were a warped parody of the mind-beamers' cries. She shuddered again, and she looked at Talisker.

"Nothing," Marvell said quietly. "It's empty!"

The planet was truly a ghost world. Bleak rock, and the glittering wreckage of age-old Plots; fused steel, hanging towers, half-built ships; buildings buried under monstrous growths; and twin moons playing a twisting light uncertainly over the surface, graying the haunted places so that the writhing shadows were menacing and the ruins fearful.

"It should be empty!" Liz heard herself say. "It's finished."

"No," said the Director.

"No?"

"No," said Marvell. He was standing upright. He had regained his courage, and he feared for the girl as well as for himself. He took her hand, and she was glad.

"It was empty," said Deneb, himself awed by the strange sight, "until about five years ago. But Spingarn set some of the Frames going. And filled them with Time-outers."

"He used Talisker! Why!"

"You can work it out, Liz," said Marvell. "He wanted to try his random principle."

"I can't—it's crazy! Random principle?"

"Yes," said Deneb.

"You'll understand soon," said the Director.

Already Liz could begin to grasp the cosmic scale of Spingarn's genius. Experiments with random probabilities! It had been possible, theoretically. Why, they'd discussed it—only as a joke of course—one day in the pre-Plotting course. *A joke?* It had happened! It wasn't enough for this hotshot Spingarn to manufacture Plots to make the Frames—not nearly enough! Somehow he had tied up the Time-outers with a random probability curve. And then used Talisker as a proving ground!

"So he should be on Talisker?" she said. "This Spingarn?"

"And a few thousand others," agreed Deneb. "No one!" he grunted as the scanners picked out the past glories of Talisker, searching for a sign of human life. "No one at all! Our scanners can home in even if it's just one man!"

"But where is he?" Liz exclaimed. "Is he back?"

The Director waved a hand and the screens were bland, blue and empty. Talisker was gone.

"His robot returned with information on the cell-structure contrivance that could reverse his experiments with the cassettes."

"The cassettes too!"

The Director ignored her question.

It was bewildering to Liz Hassell. The memory-cassettes affected by some kind of random principle? *How?* Marvell's mind was racing too.

"Spingarn sent the robot back? The Time-out Umpire he took with him? The one he found in the Time-out blip?"

"The same," agreed the Director. "One robot. Returned with information about a so-called Genekey. And it worked."

"But Spingarn! And the girl he took!"

"Missing," said Deneb.

Liz waited, lost in the exchange. Spingarn she knew of. Talisker was where the Frames had begun. The rest was an enigma. Marvell had said something to the humanoid secretary outside the office about a cell-structure change in the Director. *Bodily change—how?* She could not begin to guess. And now she was listening to an account of a robot coming back from Talisker with obviously priceless data! *Wait!* she ordered herself. Wait until a clue emerges—and then examine it carefully before coming to a conclusion.

"And the robot's back?" Marvell repeated.

"A year ago," said Deneb.

"A year! So what's Spingarn up to?" the Plot Director

demanded. "What's the robot got to say about him and the variables on Talisker?"

The Director didn't answer directly.

"I wondered about you, Marvell," he said, red wet lips pursed. "You make some maniacal blunders. But Comp says it's you and how can I argue?"

"Me?" Marvell said faintly, and Liz Hassell wondered about his lack of imagination; she squeezed his hand reassuringly. Surely he knew that he was due for a change of career?

"You," said the Director. "You, Marvell."

Deneb again tried to be reasonable.

"Look at it this way, Marvell," he said. "You're helping us all! We need your special kind of skills, man! Why, you could be another Spingarn down on Talisker! Help wind down the random element—even get through to the Alien that's causing all the—"

"Alien!"

Marvell gasped; Liz Hassell felt an emptiness inside her that was like reaching a hand through an open dark space and finding that the hand, the space beyond, and then the brain that directed the hand and the body too were somewhere beyond thought, beyond any framework of experience that she could think of. *Alien!* There had been no rumors, not the shadow of a hint! *Wait!*

"Get Spingarn's robot," ordered the Director.

Deneb moved.

"You mean *me,*" Marvell said, still openmouthed. "Me! Go to—"

"Talisker. Yes. With Miss Hassell."

Liz Hassell felt the blood drain from her face. She turned, disengaged her hand from Marvell's tight grip, and started to run: and stopped, for there, before her, was an elegant tall robot shimmering in opalescent red velvet. Bowing. Bowing for all the world like some exquisite from the Elegance Frame.

"Oh no," she whispered.

Marvell caught her as she fainted.

CHAPTER

★ 3 ★

"Is she going to do this often?" Liz Hassell heard as she opened her eyes. Marvell was half-supporting her with an expression of concern on his fleshy face; but it was the Director who had asked the question.

"I don't suppose she's seen a Time-out Umpire before," Marvell told him. "Horace must have been a shock."

Liz gagged, trying to speak.

"Feminine weakness," said the Director, with dislike. "Marvell, you're not to be envied in your mission."

"I'm all right!" Liz called, pushing Marvell's arm away and getting to her feet. She smoothed down the luxurious fur. "This *thing* startled me."

"Horace," agreed Marvell. "Spingarn's robot."

"An Umpire," the robot said, hurt. "It was my function to arbitrate on the niceties of Time-outs. I became involved in the Talisker affair purely by accident—"

"Quiet," said Deneb.

The automaton was offended. Liz could see that it was both conceited and arrogant; incredibly, too, it was vain about its appearance, for it had adopted an outer covering of a fiery, fibrous material that glowed redly with a weird, hypnotizing effect. As she smoothed the rich fur she wore, it was doing much the same to its own covering. It radiated hurt pride at Deneb's abrupt order. High-grade humanoids were temperamental beasts: so this was Spingarn's companion!

Marvell had other concerns.

"You don't need me for Talisker? You're not serious, Director? Me and the girl? Us?"

Liz adapted more swiftly to the situation. For a flaring instant she could visualize the enigmatic Spingarn—the Probability Man himself—against the haunted world of Talisker. And with this pompous, redly-glistening humanoid beside him! And to go to the lonely, deserted planet herself!

Marvell almost gobbled in dismay. The two men facing him listened to his incoherent spluttering, and then Deneb said crisply:

"All the possibilities have been worked on, Marvell. It isn't a problem for Disaster Control. Comp hasn't come up with a solution which can be sought after by any of the agencies. What it does say is that Talisker needs a man whose actions just *might* reflect those of Spingarn's—"

"But Spingarn was a maniac! He didn't act logically! He got Talisker's obsolete Frames working again! He was outside the law—"

The Director regarded him with unamused black eyes. Liz Hassell watched Marvell's expostulations die away. Marvell feared the Director.

"Listen to Horace," he told Marvell. "Horace will be going with you."

"Sir—" protested the humanoid.

Deneb glared once and it was silent.

Liz Hassell had to pinch herself surreptitiously to make sure that it was not all an involved nightmare; the pain was real enough. Yet the glistening humanoid still faced Deneb and the Director with an air of sullen rebellion, and Marvell—cigar mostly ash in his large, pudgy hand, cravat crumpled sadly, bald head covered in runnels of sweat—was almost in tears of disbelieving rage. Could it be that she was to be whirled through the spaceways far out to the Rim of the Galaxy with such unlikely companions? To a desolate, ruined mausoleum of a planet? *Her?* Liz Hassell?

"It goes by the name of Horace," the Director announced, "since that was what the Probability Man chose to call it. Horace!"

"Sir?"

"Explain your function."

A shallow mentality, thought Liz. It was amazing what

they could do with machines these days. Had some saturnine engineer built its vapid, superficial arrogance into its circuits, or was that a natural development of the thing's own electronic coils? She could smile as it postured.

"My function is to be your guide," Horace announced importantly. "I had the honor of accompanying Mr. Spingarn on his venture to the Frames of Talisker, and it is now my pleasure to have been detailed to return to the planet with yourselves."

"Dear God," whispered Marvell. "It goes with us? *That?*"

The Director smiled a death's-head's grin.

"Ask it about Talisker."

"No!" Marvell shuddered.

"Miss Haskell?"

Liz knew that she and Marvell were being played with. She could accept that too. Along with the terrifying information that she was to face the incredible emptiness of Talisker: and the thing they had called *Alien*. She was still trembling slightly, still in awe of the Director; but she would not fear him. Fear could come later.

"Why did Spingarn go to Talisker?" she asked the humanoid.

It shrugged elegant red shoulders.

"Why, to try to cancel the effects of random gene mutation."

Liz knew that the rumors were true. There had been the terrible experiment.

"And you succeeded?"

The Director glared poisonously. He said nothing.

"Of course," the humanoid said negligently.

"Horace brought back the Genekey specification," Deneb put in. "Comp used the information to reverse all known mutations."

There was a mystery she knew nothing of, she could see. It could be investigated later. For the moment, she would ask the important questions.

"What happened on Talisker?"

Deneb looked worried now.

"I accompanied Sergeant Hawk and Spingarn, with Spingarn's assistant, a female, to the surface of the planet. I returned with the Genekey specif—"

"You've said that. I know that now. Where did you find the specifications?"

"On Talisker, Miss Hassell!"

The Director was deeply amused.

"Then how did you find them?"

Marvell muttered: "Don't ask it any more. Who wants to know about Talisker? The hell with Talisker!"

"How?" Liz repeated.

The robot was piqued.

"I have no information."

"No information! Why not?"

"Because it's got more sense than you!" snarled Marvell at her. "Forget Talisker! Forget Spingarn, Liz!"

"Why no information?" persisted Liz.

The robot pointed to its furred headpiece.

"This was empty, miss. All it contained was the Genekey specification. Apart from that, nothing. I was returned to Center in a state of unknowingness, with my memory-circuits obliterated."

"It gets worse," Marvell whined. Liz felt all her dislike of him returning. "We go back to en empty planet, not knowing what to expect, with *that!*"

"What do you know?" Liz asked.

The robot shrugged.

"Before Spingarn was sent into Talisker, the most extreme of probability variables were plotted in an effort to determine what was happening there. The conclusion was that an extra-Universal agency was in operation."

"And?"

"I have no direct memories, of course, but nothing in my experience runs counter to that prediction. I conclude that an extra-Universal entity allowed me to return with the information that could reverse all cell-mutation experiments."

"Cell-mutation—" Liz began.

"You'll be informed," Deneb said abruptly. "They're not your main concern, Miss Hassell."

"Then what is my main concern?"

The Director extended his emaciated neck; his teeth shone overwhite, his black eyes regarded her with detestation.

"It seems that our selection procedures are most extraordinarily good! An incisive intellect, a woman of determination—Marvell, how fortunate you are to have such a companion!"

Marvell spat a couple of Mechanical Age obscenities at Liz Hassell; they were quaint reminders of the overwhelming importance those long-lost people placed on their bowels. There would be time enough to remind Marvell of them. She could ignore his scared vulgarity, because she was so powerfully excited by the mission for which she was detailed. Spingarn, Talisker, and *Alien*! They held her entranced, their bizarre names summoning up a universe of associations.

Nevertheless, she spoke calmly:

"Do I understand," she said, directing her question at the skinny, hating figure before her, "that we are detailed to locate Spingarn?"

There was a snarl of genuine viciousness.

"Spingarn you can bury! I don't care about the Spingarns of this or any other world!"

"Then his woman?"

"Her too!"

Marvell nodded agreement. "Her too!"

"His companion—Sergeant Hawk?"

"A destroyed psyche," Horace said. "It seems that his persona was totally overlaid by a conditioning process for use in a Gunpowder Age Plot! How it came—"

"Quiet," Deneb said once more. The robot bowed in reply. Liz was tempted to giggle at its solemn, elegant, frustrated mannerisms; she recognized an unfamiliar lack of confidence in herself now. It had to be put down.

"Would you care to tell Marvell and myself precisely *why* we are being sent to Talisker?" she said loudly. "Why us, and why go at all, sir?"

The Director was in the grip of an icy fury.

"Why reactivate Talisker in the first place?" he snarled at her. "Why does a hell-maggot like Spingarn have to build himself into every Plot in the Frames? Why does he have to set up the random variables that let him crew Talisker with the Time-outers? And when he's sent out to Talisker—to die, and quickly! Quickly!—does he have to survive? We have the Genekey, we're rid of Spingarn—Talisker isn't a danger—"

"Sir!" interrupted Deneb. "Sir, Talisker is the danger! We're still getting random variables in the established

Frames—we're still getting inexplicable happenings. It must be Talisker!"

Marvell groaned.

"Not us! Not me, anyway!"

"You!" Deneb said, while the Director gobbled noiselessly in an attempt to contain his vicious rage. "The Guardians say both you and Miss Hassell."

The Director pointed a skinny hand at them.

"Go!"

Liz shrank away from the unconcealed violence of the gesture. She was dazed, afraid and bewildered. But there burned in her mind a fierce desire to know more about the enigmatic Spingarn whom she must now follow with the reluctant Marvell. Random variables! And cell-mutation changes! It made the little Plot she had been working on with such intensity for the past months seem altogether banal. In all of her short working life she had never known this complete, almost frenzied lust for knowledge.

"Dear God!" Marvell whimpered. "He means it!"

When they were outside the great cavernous room, Liz turned to Marvell.

"It's the most wonderful thing I've ever heard of! It makes Plotting look like kids' games! Marvell, I want to go to Talisker!"

He looked at the smiling green-faced humanoid secretary.

"Dear God, she means it!"

Horace regarded Marvell with distaste.

"The Guardians are ready for you, sir. Miss?"

"If you only knew what you were letting yourself in for!" Marvell groaned. "Why pick on me? I'm too good a Director to be wasted on Talisker! I've got a new Plot running at this very minute—how is it doing?" he called over his shoulder as Horace tried to usher him away.

"A success, sir. Assistant Dyson reports an overwhelming triumph. The fliers were particularly invigorating—there was an unprecedented casualty list. May I offer my congratulations, sir?"

Marvell glared at Liz Hassell.

"And I have to leave it to Dyson! Do you know what they're going to do to us now?"

Liz grinned back at him. "I can guess. Is it memory-cassettes? We go through the sausage machine?"

"Why do you always know everything, woman?" He spoke to the robot, Horace: "Was Spingarn's woman like that?"

"A most loyal lady," Horace answered. "And, at times, a resourceful companion. At least, I believe so from the impressions that remain to me. More, alas, I cannot say. Shall we proceed?"

Deneb called them back.

"Marvell! Miss Hassell! The Director is distraught. There are good reasons, but I'll not delay you by speaking of them. I think you are both still in some doubt as to the nature of your assignment."

Marvell shook his head. "Where's the cause for doubt? We're to go to a planet that's deserted. And we're to look for someone you don't really want to find. And when we find him, we're to ask why we're there. I ask you, Deneb, doesn't it sound straightforward?"

Deneb did not respond to the irony.

"Comp says it's you to go, Marvell. They'll explain the reasoning for your selection. I have to tell you this: we're getting unaccountable Disasters all through the Frames. Comp is barely able to cope. All through the Galaxy, we're having troubles, and not just the simple kind."

"So let me stay to help solve your problems!"

Deneb carried on, unperturbed, serious and grave: "Spingarn faced the Alien and brought back the Genekey. When you contact the Alien, do as much as he did. That's your assignment. Contact the Alien entity and find some way of ironing out the random probabilities in the Frames."

Liz began to understand the immensity of the task. It was beyond all comprehension at first; simply, there had been too much information. Talk first of the half-mythical figure of Spingarn and his wild experiments in the random probability variables of the Frames had been followed by a sight of a planet like a graveyard.

And now this Alien with whom they must make contact! She felt almost kindly disposed toward Marvell; she knew herself to be the stronger of the two of them.

"Come on," she said. "Let's face the Guardians. At least when we get to Talisker we know that there are no Frames operating—we'll be in no immediate danger."

Marvell shambled forward.

"Anything Spingarn has handled is trouble! *Trouble!* I'd rather be back in that Mechanical Age Plot we started off. At least one could die believing in something credible. But Talisker! Dear God, Liz, do you know what he did to the derelict Frames there?"

Liz felt almost gay. "No! Let's find out!"

Horace was completely subdued by the time they had been wafted through the lower levels of the most sophisticated of all humanity's installations. For Horace, this descent into the deep, silent corridors was the equivalent of entering Heaven: to the red-furred automaton, the Guardians were God. Marvell was quiet too, for he had never seen the highest grades of robots before. Few knew of their existence. Liz Hassell told herself that they were simply machines, man-made like the rest of the gigantic apparatus that controlled the Frames on all the settled planets of the Galaxy; yet when the four robots came out of the shadows to face the small party, she could not help feeling that she was wrong.

No human had invented the Guardians, she was sure of it. Humanoid, functional, almost squat, they regarded the two humans and the quivering Time-out Umpire with an expression of quizzical sympathy. It came to Liz Hassell that the machines before her were what the robots themselves had built. *Guardians.* They were the ultimate authority on the operation of the Frames.

When you had a system whereby most of humanity spent most of its time in re-creations of other eras, you set up a fantastically complex series of interrelated events. So complex that they were beyond the powers of the human mind to follow. All Frames were operated—not invented—by the machines. And these must be what the machines themselves had evolved as their conscience.

"I'm Marvell," Marvell declared. "How in God's name did you select me for this crazy idea? You did the selection, didn't you?"

They looked at him for a moment.

When one of them spoke, Liz had the eerie feeling that they all spoke together. Only one set of near-lips moved, but a faint sense of repetition or echoing thoughts hung over all four dull-black frames.

"We are the Guardians," it said, as if amused at the idea. "All information comes through to these storehouses around you. Every recorded piece of data about everything known is here. When a Frame is required, the data are available to fill it out. That is the function of the machines about you. Ultimately, we provide ways of making your Frames and the Plots within them viable. Ours is not a decision-making function."

"Then get me out of here!" Marvell said. "I don't want to go to Talisker—this crazy bitch does, but let me *out!* Don't decide for me!"

Another machine spoke, just as dispassionately.

"There are occasions when we must give advice on decisions. This is one."

Horace was in an electronic trance.

Liz Hassell said firmly: "You decided that we should go to Talisker. Don't quibble about terms! You came to a decision and advised the Director accordingly. Is that right?"

"It is, Miss Hassell," the first Guardian said.

"On what grounds?"

"They won't tell you!" growled Marvell.

"We will" a third Guardian said. "We applied a statistical test of significance to the possibility of contacting the Alien. Your name came up, Miss Hassell, as one of the likelier possibilities."

"Mine! But I thought it was Marvell—"

"That lets me out!" Marvell cried. "You want her—take her! Let me get back to my fliers! Dear God, I don't know what gives on this Talisker thing, but you can keep my share!" He shook his paunch with relief in his fit of laughter. "Ho-ho, Liz! Ho-ho-ho-ho! It's you, not me! You for Spingarn's lunatic planet! You for the Alien! And me for the Battle of the Somme! I'll have a month of it! A month of mud and blood and fliers and howitzers—I'll build bombing planes, they must have had them! Bloody great bombers with smokestacks twenty feet high and a crew of hundreds!"

He almost wept in his relief.

"Your name came up too," said the first robot Guardian.

"Mine? I knew Spingarn, but not well—a mere acquaintance, an accidental friendship, not even a friendship really—I knew the fool only because we'd been in Plotting together once, before he turned mad and went to Talisker! Count me out! Liz, tell them I'm no use to them!"

Liz laughed aloud. "Oh, you fat fool! Stop blubbering, Marvell! Stop it! Listen!"

The first Guardian nodded in a friendly fashion. "On what grounds, you asked, Miss Hassell. First, you had an interest in Spingarn—there was the inquiry you made. Second, you were emotionally involved with Spingarn's closest associate, Director Marvell—"

"Emotionally involved!" gasped Liz, for the first time amazed by something the Guardians said. "Me? With him?"

"I scarcely knew Spingarn! Have I got the right name? Spingarn?" Marvell lied.

They looked at one another, fear and curiosity on Marvell's face, outrage and amazement on Liz Hassell's. She studied the broad, fleshy features and felt freshly repulsed by the ponderous nose, the heavy chins, the half-hidden eyes; for his part, Marvell noticed Liz's flushed face, her sparkling, angry eyes, and then the rise and fall of her chest. It had never struck him before that well-built women were peculiarly well-suited to display emotion. She heaved prettily.

"—and third," the Guardian proceeded, "such a liaison as yours might be appropriate for entering the Alien's Possibility Space."

"Liaison!" Liz shouted. "Liaison!"

"Exactly," the Guardian said. "It seemed, according to our math, statistically certain that a man and a woman, both sexually compatible, should engage in a sexual liaison when exposed to adverse circumstances of the kind likely to be encountered in a random probabilities situation—"

It stopped, because Liz shouted out very loudly: "Stop! You say I'm going to—to—"

"Mate," the second Guardian said.

"—to mate!—with that overweight buffoon!"

Marvell looked embarrassed.

Horace put in a caution: "You have little time, Miss Hassell, and you, sir. The Talisker ship is scheduled for eighteen hundred hours. That leaves only an hour or so for the memory-cassettes."

"*That!*" Marvell shuddered. "Do we have to go?" he pleaded hopelessly.

"Yes," the third Guardian said.

"The two of us?" Liz asked.

"Yes."

Marvell's face became cunning. "You've said we're needed to face this Alien. How do you know there *is* such a thing? Horace knows nothing—he's said as much."

Liz Hassell was again overcome by the terrifying mystery of Talisker. Shadowy and vague thoughts chased through her excited mind, pictures of the lost and lonely ruins of Talisker formed and misted into emptiness.

Talisker!

On that haunted, experimental planet there could be some inhuman, questing intelligence. In the derelict Frames of Talisker, the Alien that had supplied the Genekey still lingered!

"Spingarn met the Alien entity," the first Guardian said with an inarguable certainty.

"See," said another Guardian, and they looked.

A screen glowed, starlight blazed, Talisker loomed and Liz had the sensation of Phase, with the brain's electronic messages slightly out of key with the skull, so that she seemed to be in a hundred contiguous fields of space-time at once: they cleared, and she could see Talisker as it had appeared to Spingarn. The Guardians were showing her the probability variables of that mad place. A whirlwind of events so inextricable interwoven with planetary motions and chains of human growth—and with the ghastly *things* Spingarn had encountered—was engraved into her innermost thoughts. Blazing, sun-drenched ice caps towered and splintered. Roads—roads? Or rather rearing energy-bands—curled and vanished into chasms where vast humanoids stood about in dumb malice; engines roared across violet skies, and twin moons flitted in a pattern of insidious grace. Always, there was a random progression of events, tortuous, eerie, spasmodic, with endings and beginnings snaking into one another as the waves of a space-time Singularity vanish and appear. There was much that was made by man; and much that was not.

"Dear God!" Marvell said, appalled. "We can't face that, Liz!"

"You'll be conditioned," the fourth Guardian said. "Your robot guide was right. There is little time to prepare."

"You must go," the first Guardian said bleakly. "We have no other remedy. You must find why Talisker is empty, Director Marvell."

"And Miss Hassell must go with you," said the second. "Now."

There was another short journey through warm, silent tunnels as they were rushed by a coffin-like shuttle to the automaton-surgeon. They arrived together, both of them still in shock after seeing the images of Talisker. Liz barely noticed the skeletal surgeon-robot ushering them to a high-backed seat. She was used to the messy part of memory-cassette injection.

"Liz!" Marvell yelled. "Keep him off!"

"It's the surgeon," she told him. Hadn't he been in the Frames? Not ever? "Keep still! It doesn't hurt—not physically. Don't struggle, they'll just have to anesthetize you! Give in gracefully, Marvell—enjoy it!"

"I'm not a bloody virgin being raped! Get off, you—"

Liz was hypnotized by the sight of the glittering metal arms. They danced about her head, with the tiny bead of memory-circuiting held daintily in a thin hook of bright steel. What did it contain?

"Aaaaaargh!" Marvell yelled. "Don't let it, Liz! I'm going back to—"

He was silent as the spray hit him in the face. His eyes turned up in their fleshy pouches, his big body slumped; it was lifted easily into the chair beside Liz's.

The messy part, thought Liz. The insidious injection of one single, complex cell that gobbled up old memories and supplanted them by others: what had happened to the hundred thousand men who were now reenacting the ancient war of antiquity in the mud and gore of that distant arena was now to happen to her. The cell would smash through the tissues at the base of her skull, racing with lightning speed to the vital areas of control, speeding with the powerful knowledge of a sperm that knows it must find union and renew itself a million million million times! She felt the soft touch of a steel claw.

She shook and shivered. There would be no physical pain, but there would be a most terrible mental agony. The psyche had to absorb the new information: the old had to be destroyed. There would be conflict, fission, pain. A genetic bomb would shortly burst in her brain. And what would she be then? What possible Liz Hassell could cope with the dreadful arena of Talisker's living grave? What new persona that the machines could devise could successfully maintain an equilibrium where an Alien stalked the planet?

"A pleasant journey, miss," said the red-furred automaton watching her. There was an expression of considerable distaste on its smooth, angular features. She recalled that some robots were fastidious about the use of cassettes; they disliked the notion of restructuring the human psyche.

She smiled at its dismay as the cell struck.

The long blast of agony began.

CHAPTER

★ 4 ★

Marvell and Liz Hassell missed the long, looping journey through the spin-shafts of Center. Their gently respiring bodies were shunted in white coffin-like containers at high speed to the waiting shuttle. Within an hour, the little craft had linked with the enormous interstellar vessel that loomed like a black cliff in orbit beyond the planet that housed Center. Then the two voyagers were transferred into pods filled with the clinging, comforting gray ooze which was to cushion them against the disagreeable shocks of Phase. Horace followed elegantly.

The little shuttle fell away.

Deneb, who had come to watch, saw the great interstellar ship begin to shimmer as its gigantic force-fields strained against the confines of Euclidean space. It shimmered, hesitated against mighty, invisible barriers, and then vanished.

It blasted its way through blossoming suns, plunged in and out of mad vortices of warped space and time, guided by robots who were programmed to hasten the ship's voyage, no matter at what material cost. Marvell and Liz missed too the blank and terrifying reaches of space-time between the spiraling arms of the Galaxy as the ship leaped out into the gulfs where tiny shards of new matter occasionally spilled through the gaps in the island universes's dimensions. The robots expertly spun the black vessel around the dangerous, unreal arenas, preserving their human cargo for the stranger unrealities beyond.

Liz Hassell yawned, stretched and raised herself onto one elbow. She blinked twice at the dull glare of the dying red sun that shone through layers of orange haze. There was a feeling of time somehow spent, a time of fitful dreaming; otherwise, the last thing she could recall with any clarity was the sight of Marvell struggling against the surgeon-robot. She shaded her eyes against the sunlight. Two things were immediately apparent. The place where they had been set down was an extremely ordinary bit of green and quiet countryside; and she herself was still Liz Hassell. It was the second of these that was most important, of course. It might be that there were unpleasant surprises hidden just beyond the gentle, undulating curves of green meadows; in the beech and oak copse, there could lurk some unnameable monstrosity, a thing conjured up by Spingarn's meddling fingers; and the little stream that oozed its way between the banks a few yards away might also shelter tiny malevolences. Liz expected no less. It was to be assumed that Talisker would house frightfulness on a vast scale.

Meanwhile, her own psyche was intact. So was her body; she looked at herself approvingly. It was a handsome frame, well-fleshed, firm, in good condition. She patted her black hair and was pleased. The trouble with the sausage machine at Center was that it could—and often did—enforce physical changes to enable a subject to cope with the demands a particular Plot might make on him or her. If the stories were not lying rumors, Spingarn had been the victim of his own meddling when *he* had been sent to Talisker to remedy the discord there. Liz laughed aloud. She had not been transmogrified—and neither had Marvell.

Her laugh barely impinged on his consciousness. It brought Horace hurrying back, however. Within five seconds of the first signs of returning consciousness on the part of the two humans—one of them, anyway—the furred red automaton returned from his inspection of the terrain.

"Welcome to Talisker, Miss Hassell!" Horace said.

"Welcome yourself," Liz told it. "Try not to adopt an air of superior knowledge or enlightenment, will you?" She did not wait for an answer. The trouble with this kind of machine was that it did know a good deal more than any human, and it would almost certainly be capable of making better reasoned decisions: it was as well to make one's position clear at the outset. The robots soon pressed home an advantage. "Where have you been?" she demanded.

"Why, exercising my function as guide, miss!" it said, hurt. "I thought a short perambulation—"

"And you found what?"

The sun was sinking fast. The air was chill now. Liz could see beads of dew on Marvell's ridiculous hat. He was snoring with a dull sound, mouth half-open, eyes occasionally shifting beneath the lids; he looked like a great lazy sea cow, a bewhiskered and gross creature. Liz shuddered. *He* should have been fined down by the sausage machine. She recalled Dyson's slim elegance with a pang. Horace considered his answer as she stared at Marvell.

"I found surprisingly little, miss," the robot announced. "It seems that we have been set down in a backwater. There are none of the major Frames boundaries nearby, and I could find no sign of dwellings or industry. There are tracks in that direction," he said, indicating the path of the orange haze, "but not roads. Miss Hassell, this part of Talisker is empty. Should I awaken Director Marvell?"

"No." Liz felt cold as a slight wind came from the east. "Not yet. Find somewhere for us to sleep tonight. And get food ready."

The robot looked at Marvell. "Perhaps it would be better if—"

"Now!"

"Yes, miss."

It loped off, an offended automaton. Liz kicked Marvell in the ribs as soon as Horace had disappeared into the gloom. Marvell sputtered and, as she kicked again, roared out in pain.

"What! What are you doing?"

He got to his feet with a speed that surprised Liz. She had no time to get in a third kick.

"Christ!" said Marvell, ignoring her and the reason for her assault. "We're there—here! It really happened—and you're here too! Oh, dear God, they've done it!" He suddenly reached a hand to the back of his neck. "Christ!" he exploded. "My head—it hurts! That machine—those lunatics of robots! They sent me through cell-recycling. Me! Marvell!"

"It didn't work."

Marvell frowned. "It didn't. Spingarn's got a hand in it! That cunning bastard's deliberately left us alone!"

"You've got a persecution mania about Spingarn, Marvell. He couldn't have planned it—no!"

"So why are you still the scheming bitch you always were? Why not a memory recycling for you? Or me," he added as an afterthought.

Liz shrugged.

"Don't let it worry you. I'm quite sure there are going to be serious worries and soon." She was struck by Marvell's unhappy look. "Don't tell me this is the first time for you! Not the first time in the Frames?"

Marvell grimaced.

"Hated them! Always have! The main reason I went for Direction was to keep free of the Frames!"

"Why?"

Marvell was indignant.

"I loathed the idea of playing a part—why should I be anything but me—*me!*"

"Well, you egocentric clown, Marvell!" said Liz. But she felt uncertain about her judgment. "So that was why you kicked up so much when they slipped you the memory-cell. Your first time!"

"The first time!" Marvell groaned. "And look what I get! I'm cold, hungry and frightened, Christ, and I'm stuck with an infuriating bitch like you!" He looked around and took in the nature of the surroundings. "And look at it! Fields! Trees! Not a building in sight! Where am I going to sleep? And what am I going to eat?" He swatted an insect. "And bugs!"

He looked about him in disgust. His clothes hung disheveled about his large frame. His bald head wrinkled as he shivered at the cold wind that blew strongly now. The trees had a threatening appearance, gnarled branches took on eerie shapes. As the sun's disc disappeared, the light decreased rapidly; two moons began to wriggle over the horizon, though they were more like shifting, unreal phantoms than celestial bodies.

"I'm not built for the outdoor life!" Marvell groaned.

"Do something, Liz—you're my assistant, get food! Get a bed for me!"

Liz looked at the shivering man with a measure of contempt. How could such a large man be so poor-spirited?

"Oh, you poor sod," she said. "Here's Horace. With food, if I'm not mistaken."

Horace appeared carrying a rough-woven mat bulging with greenery. Over his shoulder, Liz could make out the form of a lifeless animal. Its white-specked legs swayed as Horace hefted it over his thin shoulder. Marvell watched in horror.

"Liz!" he got out. "Liz, what's that mad robot up to? He's killing— Liz, the thing's gone berserk!" He looked about for a place of sanctuary. "Liz!"

Horace paid no attention to the outburst. The robot addressed itself to Liz Hassell:

"I regret that I was unable to find suitable accommodation for the night. There are buildings, but they are at some considerable distance from here. I saw the roofs in the far distance. I would respectfully suggest that for tonight, anyway, you stayed here." He indicated the dead creature. "The flesh is edible, miss. And I have acquired sufficient fruit and vegetables to make a satisfactory meal."

"Very good, Horace," said Liz.

"Very good?" Marvell muttered, looking from one to another. "Very good?" He shuddered at the sight of a trickle of dark blood that came from the little deer's throat. "Christ, I can't eat that! You don't expect me to eat—flesh!"

"You won't get anything else," Liz pointed out.

"I've never eaten raw flesh—raw food!"

"You haven't done very much, have you?" Liz said placidly. "Horace, get firewood. And after that, make us some sort of shelter—branches, with a covering of some sort. You can do that?"

"Certainly, miss!" Horace hesitated. "I am not able to supply bio-mass, miss. Director Marvell will appreciate that I have my instructions?"

Marvell sat down shaking his head sadly.

"Dear Christ," he said. "Instructions too?"

"Get moving," Liz told the robot. To Marvell she said

crisply: "I expect its instructions are that we have to live off the land—no artificial foods, no transport devices, and quite possibly no weapons. Center wants us to use our own initiative, with only a certain amount of assistance from Horace. He can hunt, it seems, but not make the pap we live on usually." She smiled. "Can you skin this?" she said, indicating the still-warm body.

Marvell looked away, shuddering afresh.

Horace provided a sharp knife, though Liz insisted on doing the butchery of the carcass. Marvell tried to stack dried twigs and branches until Horace took time off from interweaving birch branches for their shelter to make a fire. By the time the steaks were sizzling on the ends of pointed sticks, the twin moons were well up in the violet-black sky. There was no sense of danger, no feeling of apprehension in Liz's mind. No night-calls disturbed the air. The wind, which had freshened considerably for an hour, dropped to a slight breeze that was enough to build long trails of sparks from the fire. Marvell watched first Liz, who turned the steaks, and Horace, who had almost completed a rough hut. Liz passed a stick to Marvell.

"Eat," she said. "It's burned on the outside, but you'll find it good and red after the black bit."

"Oh Christ," whispered Marvell, holding the stick as if it would attack him.

"Eat it!"

"No!"

"Try some of these."

Liz passed the green fruits and the vegetables. Marvell groaned afresh.

"Then starve!" Liz told him. She moved closer to the fire and sat munching the steaks with great pleasure. Marvell watched for a few minutes.

"Horace!" he called.

"Sir?"

"No real food?"

"None, sir. I am programmed to be able to offer the planet's normal facilities only. Unfortunately, sir, we have been deposited in a primitive area which supported an agricultural community. There is no obvious sign of advanced civilization about here."

Marvell stared at the meat he had rejected.

"It isn't hygienic," he said, undecided. "It'll be full of harmful bugs—no processing at all!"

Liz smiled.

"Try it."

He accepted the offer and nervously bit into the meat. In the bright firelight, Liz saw his expression change from nervous horror to hunger. He ripped a piece off and swallowed.

"It's gritty and foul," he said. "But it is food."

He ate an unripe apple after several pieces of steak. Liz fell to looking out at the stars as Marvell finished his meal. She was a little abstracted, but that was not unexpected. Powerful drugs had held the two of them in a state of slightly euphoric unconsciousness during the long journey to the Rim and Talisker, with its twin gyrating moons. There would be residual traces of the drugs. Was that why they had been set down in this peaceful backwater, with its harmless green countryside and its ready food supplies? To give them a day of orientation?

"I don't like it," Marvell said, when he was through eating.

"What?"

"It's all too easy! No sign of anything but this overgrown garden! It's unnatural! Talisker's supposed to be dangerous! Horace!"

"Sir?"

"Is it dangerous?"

Horace pondered the matter.

"I could guess about the inherent possibilities of the situation. I still have my deductive facilities, sir."

"So go on!"

"Well, sir, if we examine the static elements of the situation, we soon come up against a high degree of certain probabilities."

"Be precise, Horace! Enough of your robotic jargon! You're not talking to another bloody machine!"

The red-gold fur on the carapace of the robot shivered with disgust. Liz saw that Horace detested Marvell's crude expletives.

"*Very* well, sir," it said, a world of pointed distaste in its tones. "You have been advised to—"

"Advised! Forced into this bloody mad world!"

"—advised to follow Mr. Spingarn and his party to

Talisker to discover whether or not the apparently deserted condition of the planet has any relationship with the hypothetical Alien presence."

"Yes," said Liz. She looked out at the few stars again. Other island universes made those brightly glowing white-blue spangles in the sky, for Talisker swam a solitary course at the far edge of the Galaxy. *Alien!*

How had it arrived here?

"Well, sir, and Miss Hassell," the robot went on, "the fact that you are both in command of your own personae, that is," he said with a glance at Marvell's lowering face, "because you are both yourselves still, is no indication that you will *remain* so. And because there is apparent security hereabouts is no indication that there is no danger. You see, the Laws of Probability won't function with a high Certainty Quotient, not on Talisker."

Liz felt a strange sense of frightened wonder, much the same as she had felt when she saw the fliers on the ancient piece of battle film; Horace was promising a random situation. It didn't seem possible, not when they sat on the patch of dry grass around the blazing fire, not when the night sky above them was filled with splendid, isolated star systems, and two crazy moons waltzed about thin, high clouds. She recognized that she had experienced only a sense of anticlimax up to that moment. All the speculation and amazement she had undergone when the strange adventure was thrust on her had almost been dissipated. It returned with a sweeping nerve-shaking power.

"Make it simple for a simple man," complained Marvell. He picked meat from his teeth with a twig.

"Yes, sir." Horace was a skeletal red ghost in the firelight. "Cell-fusion hasn't taken place yet in your brains, neither yours nor Miss Hassell's. It could do so at any moment—any time that there was a need for you to adapt to one of Talisker's Frames."

"So we're waiting," said Liz slowly. "We're waiting with a genetic time-bomb in here." She felt the back of her head. There was a tiny needle of pain as she pressed at the base of her skull, though she might have imagined it.

"Christ," said Marvell, yawning. "That's all I need. The back of my head ready to explode. I suppose Spingarn would find it funny. I wonder where he is."

Marvell looked uneasily into the darkness.

There was enough moonlight to illuminate the trees and the low sweep of the hills. They were gray-green in the bright whiteness. Liz thought of the strange sights she had seen in the Director's screens, back at Center: beyond the low hills were the ruins of all Talisker's experimental, haunted Frames.

"Spingarn, sir?" said Horace. "I've given the matter thought. I am of the opinion that both he and his companions—a lady called Ethel and a destroyed psyche who goes by the name of Sergeant Hawk—will be found when we come into contact with some of the random situations set up by the Alien. That's my assessment of the probabilities at the moment."

"Random situations set up by the Alien?" repeated Liz. "You think this hypothetical Alien has emptied Talisker?"

Horace's face showed sardonic amusement.

"I don't believe that Talisker is empty, miss! Oh, no! The Probability Quotient for Talisker having been depopulated is very low indeed!"

"But we *saw* the place was empty!" Liz protested. "We saw nothing on the screens—not a sign of human life!"

"Quite, miss," the robot agreed.

Marvell sensed the quiet satisfaction in the automaton's high-pitched voice.

" 'Not a sign—' " he repeated. "You said there wasn't a sign of—"

"Human life," said Liz slowly. "No human life." She and Marvell scanned the darkness. There were shapes in the darkness. Tussocks of grass seemed to edge nearer; small, isolated bushes grew menacing protuberances; the slight wind brought a sighing noise from the beeches. "If not human life, then what?"

"This Alien," said Marvell, breaking a long silence. "Don't you recall anything about it? Where it came from, what it's doing here, what it *wants*?"

Horace was enjoying himself.

"I was able to read Spingarn's accounts, sir—though my memory-banks were wiped clean of all that occurred while I accompanied Mr. Spingarn on my first visit to Talisker, I was instructed by, the, ah, Guardians," and his voice was reverent, "to scan the reports of the expedition. The bare facts, as it were. It seems that the Alien presence, if there *is* one here, is unsure of its function. It seems to be in much the same circumstances as yourself and Miss Hassell, sir."

"Christ," said Marvell with feeling.

"Lost," said Liz. "It's lost?"

"So my interpretation of the Probability Quotient would suggest," agreed the robot. "Yes, miss, lost."

"I've had enough for one day," Marvell said briskly. "I need sleep. Riddles don't interest me anymore. Alien! Little lost Alien! Dear Christ, I wish I could get back to civilization! I'm probably crawling with diseases. Is that hut free of bugs?" he demanded of Horace.

"Entirely habitable, sir. You rest on the dried bracken."

"Liz?" asked Marvell, noting her well-rounded figure.

"If I must! But keep away from me!"

Marvell shrugged.

"It wouldn't be hygienic anyway."

Liz repressed an urge to giggle. Marvell was too much. The hotshot Director obsessed with sanitation—and a planet that was empty but not empty. And a thing from outside the Universe, lost on Talisker.

She fell asleep watching the glitter of stars through the tiny gaps in the interwoven branches.

CHAPTER

★ 5 ★

Dawn brought a blast of noise from thousands of birds. Liz awoke to find that she and Marvell had moved closer during the night; his bulk impinged on her. She recalled that she had been grateful for the warmth of his large body. The whistling, shrieking, calling and croaking of the birds reminded her of their mission. They were on Talisker. *The robot.* Where was it?

She crawled out of the makeshift shelter on hands and knees. Scores of birds in the nearby copse erupted in flight as she emerged. She grinned. In the soft furs she habitually wore, she must look like some predator. Behind her, Marvell moaned in his sleep.

There was no sign of the robot.

The ashes of last night's fire swirled in the light wind; it was dawn, with red-pink glows just below the horizon. The moons were down. It would be a fine day. The birds shrilled louder as she got to her feet.

"Horace!" she called loudly. "Horace!"

Mist swirled over the little brook. She realized that she was thirsty. Dirty too, with fingers greasy still from the fat of the deer. She ran her fingers through her fine black hair and felt matted twists; a flea ran down her bare arm. She shuddered and ran to the brook.

The wet grass sparkled under her bare feet; it was cold, but invigorating. Where was Talisker's danger? It was almost like being back in the kind of Primitive Frames she delighted in—there was the challenge of close contact with natural things, civilization was a Galaxy away. The birds were suddenly quiet.

"Miss Hassell!" shrilled a high-pitched voice. "Miss Hassell—stop! Stop!"

Liz turned as she ran, recognizing the urgency of the robot's yell. She caught a glimpse of the red-gold skeletal figure bursting through the copse; she knew why the birds were quiet; in the same instant she knew that the planet that Spingarn had filled with his Time-outers was not harmless as it had seemed in the dawn mist; and she was aware too that something below the ground was heaving her aside just as she reached the slow-running brook. A ripple in the wet grass, a sudden increase in the wind's strength, a shuddering of even the crisp morning air, all told her that electromagnetic forces had become aware of her presence.

"Marvell!" she called, as the ground fell away below her.

"Grasers!" Horace was shrilling. "Graser-mines, Miss Hassell!"

Liz scarcely heard, for the air was bending into its constituent atoms and molecules; bright flashes sparkled in front of her eyes; brighter gleams smashed inside her head as space was warped to allow the passage of her body. Suddenly she was a hundred feet above the makeshift night-shelter. There was no sign of Marvell, she told herself numbly as a mighty force tore at her body and spun her in a new direction. End over end she tumbled, her thoughts scattering away from her in the complex, gyrating patterns she was describing high above the surface of Talisker; she saw, in the distance, the ruined towers of a city of some kind. Again, when she had been shot high into the thin air she saw that the little patch of greenery below her was a parkland set in a patchwork of arenas; there was a village, a couple of hamlets, and outlying buildings, little more. And all around the parkland was a great, shimmering swath of blackness. If she could have made sense of the situation, she would have found it intriguing. *Graser-mines?* And then she had to fight for breath as a lurching, sideways movement shot her higher still, into the rarefied regions where the atmosphere was almost at an end; she could see the curve of Talisker's horizon distinctly, for the sun was climbing beyond the disc's edge. Clouds swam below her, and still the thrust of—*grasers?*—took her. Liz gasped and felt particles of ice in her eyelids. Was the bloody thing trying to force her into orbit over this mad planet? *Grasers*—she had heard of grasers, but what did that matter when she was swept down in the grip of this titanic force? Down, down, she went, drawing great lungfuls of breath and closing her eyes against the speed of the descent. The ground lurched below her, the greenery of that deceptive bit of Talisker. And then she was on the ground again, shaking still, eyes stinging and lungs heaving.

Horace bent over her.

"I must apologize for my lapse in failing to warn you of the possibility of graser-mines," he was saying. "I was unable, however, to give you such a warning since the terms of my commission don't allow advance information about the various probabilities—"

Marvell emerged from the shelter rubbing his eyes. Automatically he smoothed the large black moustache and placed the battered top hat on his bald head.

" 'Morning, Liz," he called. "Sleep well?" To the robot he said: "*Now* have you located some real food?"

Liz could not speak, for she was still panting.

"I'm afraid not, sir."

"Get up, Liz," ordered Marvell. "I want something to eat. It looks as though we're here for a day or two—we'll have to make some effort to find what's happening, enough to satisfy the Director. Come on, Liz!"

Liz recovered. She realized that it was of little use showing indignation. Calmly she said:

"Don't try to get water. The brook's mined."

"Mined?" he said, alert now.

"Graser-mine," Liz told him. "It caught me. Horace couldn't warn me—us."

Marvell inspected the robot, which wore a look of apology.

"It gets worse," he said at last. "You, Liz, you trod on a graser?" He looked up at the dawn. "It got you?"

"Not for long."

"I was able to cut off the power-source," Horace said modestly. "A small application of energy at the right moment."

Marvell shivered with cold.

"You were lucky, Liz. Grasers get you and hold you—but grasers! Here! I thought this was a bit of Primitive! And the place is *mined*? It doesn't fit in with the Frame factors—grasers are advanced technology, certainly post-Steam Age."

Liz remembered. "Grasers," she said. "Lasers, grasers. Gravity—grasers. The planet's force-fields—yes. Twenty-first or twenty-second century maybe, or later still. They were the basis of the first Phase ships."

"Interesting toys," said Marvell. "Mines! Lucky you weren't flipped into orbit."

"I nearly was." Liz shivered. She was annoyed with the robot, irrationally of course, because it could do no other than let them make mistakes. It was clear enough about its orders. It could not interfere with any decisions either of them made: clear up the mess afterward, not move to avoid their making one. "I'm thirsty," she complained. "And I feel foul!"

"Yes, miss," said the robot. *Was it laughing at her?* Liz had no time for anger, for Marvell was fastening his frock coat. He bent to adjust the bright yellow spats.

"Come on," he told Liz. "We're not staying here."

"We're not—" she said, surprised. It was the first time that Marvell had given an order. She got to her feet.

"We move!" Marvell said, fumbling in his pocket for cigar-case and matches. "You don't think they planted the grasers for fun?" He looked about the fields, where the mist was clearing. "Horace—get us clear! No, Liz," he said, turning to her, "whatever this Frame's about, it's *nasty*. Tricky—I feel it here," he said, placing a hand on his swelling stomach. "Minefields—there'll be minefields under the minefields! That's how *I'd* build a Frame around the grasers!"

Liz speculated hurriedly. It was obvious that Marvell took the little patch of territory to be some kind of arena. She would not ask him, since he had almost ignored her late predicament.

"I want to eat," she told him. "Eat, bathe, drink."

"Later!"

He walked away, with Horace leading. The robot adjusted his skeletal limbs so that they formed the interstices of a parabolic scanner; twice during the long trek it avoided a beaten path. Liz was careful to walk where

Marvell and Horace had trodden. She was still shaky after her abrupt ascent into the blue-violet haze above the planet, though she would not have admitted it to Marvell; the robot she discounted. Marvell seemed to have found reserves of energy from somewhere; he was more like his familiar, braggart and overconfident self. White-gray smoke curled back to Liz, rich and pungent, from his cigar; he looked like some bedraggled dignitary fallen on hard times but aware of his intrinsic importance.

Horace stopped after they had been walking for over an hour.

"Buildings," the robot said. "It's a large farm, sir." He concentrated, and Liz could almost feel the probing scanners that searched the ground. "Nothing here, sir, nothing that could cause you and Miss Hassell any danger."

Liz saw whitewashed interiors, a stone-tiled roof, high windows and gray stone outbuildings. There were simple machines, clearly horse-drawn, in the yard. Chickens watched with interest. There was a growling sound from one side of the house. A white and black bitch sidled toward them.

"A dog!" announced Marvell. "Here, ah, boy!"

The bitch bounded forward at the invitation.

"It's a deserted farm," Liz said aloud, but really to herself. "It's a farm! There'll be water—water!"

She patted the collie bitch and walked on faster.

"If there's any real food, Liz—" called Marvell.

"Find it yourself!" she shouted, running.

Inside, there was brass and clean whitewash, heavy oak beams, solid pine furniture, an oil lamp hanging from the ceiling—a wonderful re-creation of some lost farming setting. Liz found a bathroom. There was a shower, with cold, clear water from a tub on a shelf. She stripped, bathed, drinking from the showering water as she soaped herself. As she scrambled through a linen closet for towels, she caught the first scents of the breakfast Horace was cooking.

"Oh!" she gasped. "Food!"

They were on the road again an hour later. Walking, for there was no transport. Liz wanted to wring the necks of a couple of chickens so that they would be able to eat later, but Marvell had turned green at the idea. And so, carrying a small hamper filled with the tinned foodstuffs they had found at the farm ("You can't call it stealing," Marvell had said, helping himself. "We're trying to find what happened to *them*, and they won't argue if they feed us in the process."), Horace led them to the edge of the little arena that was some kind of re-creation of an earlier reality.

They knew it was the end of the Frame, because their way was blocked.

"I saw it!" Liz exclaimed as they topped a steep rise and faced the unreal black, glittering barrier before them.

"Horace?" invited Marvell.

It rose sheer into the sky. Higher than Liz had realized, it dominated the terrain, oscillating gently in the breeze, and stretching from one side of the small horizon to the other. Impossibly, it was grounded in a mist-like vapor, so that the whole structure seemed to hang a little above the ground on a frill of lace.

"I know," said Liz. "It's a Frame boundary."

"And beyond?"

"I can't remember—I only caught glimpses. I thought a ruined city complex, maybe not."

Marvell pushed his hat back.

"They'd have parceled the whole surface of the planet out," he mused. "Used the entire land and water area by the time they'd worked through all the material they wanted to try out. You know, they kept Talisker going for nearly two centuries as a proving ground, before it got Ancient Monument status. Spingarn was Curator, did you know?"

"Yes," said Liz.

"Horace?" said Marvell again.

"Sir?"

Marvell pointed. "This. I'm not going back *there*," he said, indicating the inviting green terrain behind them. "I'm not being batted about in graser-mazes. You never can tell with these old force-fields," he went on. "Get a kink in them, and they can separate you into bits you wouldn't know yourself as." He smiled as Liz tried not to shiver. She still felt moments of vertigo at the memory of those frantic seconds above Talisker. "Now, Horace, we're stuck here till Center realizes we can't help. Get us over that."

Horace seemed to ponder the matter for a few seconds.

"You're quite sure that you wish to do so, sir?" he asked. Liz looked back and saw the collie bitch.

Marvell nodded.

"Over. Through. Beyond. Now."

"Wait," said Liz. She waved to the bitch which came nearer. "Give us a run-down on the probabilities of finding the Alien if we do," she told Horace.

"Good dog," Marvell said as the bitch came up to them. "Horace?"

Horace frowned.

"I have a dim feeling I've encountered this situation before, sir. I may be wrong. Memory-erasure is fairly efficient in such cases as my treatment, but there can be hints locked up in the circuits."

"Well?"

"My best guess is that Miss Hassell is both right and wrong."

"That's Liz," agreed Marvell complacently.

"The right first," Liz said, fondling the bitch. It looked sleek and well-fed, but it was frightened. She thought suddenly of the absence of people. It was lonely. The robot interrupted her speculations.

"Yes, miss," said Horace. "I'd estimate that we're at the junction of two separate Frames, as Miss Hassell suggests. On one side we have a reenactment of reality based on an agricultural community, which had some odd sidelights. And on the other side of the barrier, there will be quite a different area of re-creation. Originally, there would have been a complete physical separation between the Frames, with this barrier as a *cordon sanitaire*."

"Now the wrong," said Marvell. "There's interaction?"

"Oh, *yes*, sir! Graser-mines wouldn't be appropriate to a pre-Steam Age Frame! My guess, considering the Probability Quotients and plotting them on a full probability curve, is that where Frames touch one another they've at some time been subject to Frame-Shift."

"No," said Marvell, who was in fact agreeing. "Graser-mazes are an early Third-Millennium game. Frame-Shift, eh?"

"I'm not sure what that is," said Liz.

Marvell smiled.

"I thought you knew everything."

"You're the one that knew Spingarn. Maybe he told you more than you admitted to the Director."

Marvell reacted with a sullen impatience.

"So why should I put myself up a tree? Spingarn did tell me about Frame-Shift!"

Liz waited, but it was the robot who explained.

"I think, sir—I establish from my readings of the probability curve—that if you, ah, we, tried to get over the barrier, it would move us along."

"Go on," said Marvell.

"We're intruders, sir, and the barriers are programmed to apprehend intruders. Normally, if anyone in a particular Frame tried to get over the barrier, he'd be picked up for interrogation and possible return to his own environment."

"And if we tried it?" asked Liz.

"Interrogation centers won't be operational on a museum-planet," said Marvell. "Horace?"

The robot was allowed to continue.

"If Frame-Shift occurs when we're on the barrier, miss, it would be exceedingly dangerous."

"Yes, Horace?"

"Frame-Shift means that any one or more of the Frames could crumble at any time. And if you and Mr. Marvell are on the barrier at such a moment, it would be regrettable."

Marvell was intrigued.

"It really could happen, Liz. Spingarn said—" He stopped.

"I thought you knew," she said.

Marvell shrugged.

"He was a bastard, but he *did* things! He said he'd seen a mountain chain, ice caps and all, reduced to a flat desert in seconds. Total destruction. Total shift of strata. You have to keep away from the barriers—that's where you get maximum risk."

Liz gulped.

"It could happen here?"

"You heard Horace. Now do you see why I wasn't going to be a hero?"

Liz patted the bitch.

"Well, what can we do?"

Marvell watched the great black mass shimmering in the morning sunlight. Then he grinned.

"Horace!"

"Sir?"

"You said you could use local resources in our service?"

"Yes, sir."

"Get us over the barrier."

"I'm not permitted to use my own energy-fields—"

Liz felt her heart begin to pound with excitement. She knew that Marvell's complex and tortuous imagination had been at work.

"The grasers! Dig a graser-mine up and program it for limited range—but get us over!"

Liz admired the dexterity of the robot in the next few minutes. It was easy enough to locate the fairly simple devices buried at intervals about the farm, but it took considerable ingenuity to redesign their antique controls. Long coils of entrail-like tubes that emitted a phosphorescent-like radiation hung about Horace's great gaunt arms; yards of the stuff had to be knitted into a trelliswork of branches he had put together; yet with some speed the work went forward. The bitch watched with interest.

At last Horace said: "The conveyance is ready, sir."

"It's a safe ride?" Marvell said, apprehensive again.

"Almost a hundred percent," Horace said. "There could be a small uncertainty element, but it's very slight."

Marvell smiled greasily at Liz. She noticed that he had neither washed nor shaved at the farm.

"You first, Liz!"

"No!"

Marvell noticed the black and white collie bitch.

"We could try him."

"Her!"

"Her then."

"No!" snarled Liz, angry now. "You!"

"Christ, what an assistant I have!"

He gestured to Horace. The robot pointed to a slight dip in the ground a few yards from the barrier. "If you would stand there, sir?"

"Grasers! That I've lived to get caught up in early Third-Millennium technology!" Marvell complained. "Liz, don't say I didn't warn—"

Horace had thrown circuits together, and Marvell's bulk was pitched upward with incredible speed.

"Miss?" suggested Horace.

The bitch struggled as she urged it forward. Liz felt confused. All she could think of was the collie's fears. What sort of people had been living in this dangerous, green bit of re-created reality? How had Spingarn's Timeouters existed among the minefields of the Primitive Frame? Who would wish to live in momentary expectation of a sudden lift into the stratosphere? The collie growled at her. She released it and then the ground fell away as bright sparks banged into her eyes and she was hurtling upward, the bitch watching her in panic, her brain full of tiny arrows as force-fields rang around her. The descent was as unpleasant as before.

Marvell was already on his feet, eyes shining with awed incredulity.

"Liz! Christ, let's go back! Liz, it's not for us!"

Liz looked and saw that Talisker had played another grim trick on them. Beyond this barrier was a fearsome sight. By some bizarre trickery, they were about to descend into a shimmering desert land, flat and frightening. What lay in the desert was worse.

Liz understood Marvell's yell. The haunted planet showed itself in its eerie strangeness. There would be no more waiting, no more playfulness.

Liz and Marvell knew that Spingarn had met the Alien.

The evidence was before them.

This was nothing to do with the Frames, experimental or otherwise. The Frames were only a realization of the ultimate form of escape. Books—films—sensors—complete total experience—and finally the Frames. The Savior of Civilization, whose dress Marvell copied as a tribute, had shown the way: move the tribes of the Americans to Europe, the tribes of the Germans to Spain, the tribes of the English to Switzerland and permutate the combinations endlessly. Always move people into different experiences, though. Use trains, then aircraft, then spaceships.

The Frames were a logical extension of the Mechanical Age's exploitation of the means of mass travel. Now, whole populations moved to new areas of experience. New worlds—new re-created worlds were manufactured for them. And it had all begun on Talisker.

Liz's mouth was dry.

Whatever had left the monstrous blotch on the desert had not begun anywhere in the Universe.

She was set down softly.

"Marvell!" she called.

"Christ!" Marvell groaned. "Dear Christ!"

CHAPTER

★ 6 ★

There could be no doubt about it. Playtime was over. Liz Hassell could recall, with a shiver of fear, the effect produced on her by her first sight of the lost planet of Talisker when she had seen the desolation revealed by the scanners. The planet had seemed to be only the shade of a mausoleum, so remote had it been from humanity.

For miles around the flat desert, the irregular flowing lines of force radiated in unholy tendrils of fiery brilliance. It was *alien*, blankly and stupendously *alien*, through and through shot with whorls and schemes of power that left the mind reeling in confusion; no human had had a hand in the exploitation of these dreadful bands of energy—whatever grotesque forces Talisker had hinted at paled into insignificance beside the promise of *otherness* here!

This was the reason for their long, hurried flight through interstellar space: the Guardians' intention, the Director's mysterious instructions. This was the goal.

"Christ, Liz," said Marvell softly, shielding his eyes from the glare.

It was a living machine, so much Liz could work out. There was a wild tracery of creation, power and life, but it had all gone wrong! It was what the Alien had built out here at the Rim of the Galaxy, but not what the Alien had intended. The vast seas of power were in a tormented uncertainty of aim: where there should have been a central and overall design—however incomprehensible to the human mind—there was chaos. Liz felt that she was looking into the blackest reaches of uncreated space, far down a long tunnel where pre-creation writhed and struggled for birth, where universes struggled to erupt into the order of existence, where formless entities clawed for expression! It was the edge of black night!

She gasped in wonder at the hypnotic blast of powers; within the structure—it was a structure, it had been built and then demolished, but *built*, with a distinct purpose—there were schemes for transmuting matter. Liz could trace parts of purposeful activity in the subtle, confusing whorls of radiance. She watched the strange dance of molecular patterns and again she gasped as the chains of human existence were flailed into new shapes: gene-chains grew, flowered, were transmuted almost playfully.

Marvell was aghast. His face was red and serious, his neck and whole head pouring sweat; he had removed the rusty, battered top hat, with its grease stains and distinct hole. He was breathing fast. The cigar rolled around his wide lips, chewed to a rag. Liz could almost smell fear. His mouth worked with difficulty, but she could make out the words.

"Time-out!" Marvel was whispering. "For Christ's sake, Time-out!"

And still Liz marveled at the eerie sight. There had been a center, it was clear. The shimmering remains of a square, monolithic building or mass of rock itself appeared in the midst of the tumult of forces; and there was a hint of effort, of continuity somewhere inside it, if only one could reach out to understand it. She was dimly aware too of Horace's pedantic voice lecturing to Marvell: the alien presence was stronger.

"Time-out, sir?" Horace was saying to Marvell. "I'm afraid not, sir, not under any circumstances! As a former authority on Time-out rulings, I have to rule your request inadmissible!"

"It's real!" Marvell was saying to himself. "It isn't a part of this place—I can't understand *that*—I'm no Spingarn! They're mad to send me out here!" His voice rang out, and Liz could hear him. "Nobody can face a thing like *that*—no one! It doesn't fit any Frame I've ever seen or heard of—why, it isn't human! It could never be human!"

"No," said Liz. "It belongs to the Alien."

"There's no such thing!" Marvell said, shaking his large

head. "It was all Spingarn's idea! He was lying! This *thing*—it's something the machines made!"

He looked at Liz.

She had no help for him.

"No, Marvell. We've found it. Or it's found us—I think we've come across what Spingarn called the Genekey. Horace?"

"Would you like me to plot the Probability Quotients?"

"Plot away!" said Marvell, groaning.

"It almost certainly *was* the Genekey, extrapolating from available evidence," said Horace. "There are energy-fields warped in non-Universal combinations, sir. Nothing radiating from the epicenter relates to any data I have."

"Christ!"

Liz looked again at Marvell and considered him with what she hoped was an unbiased eye. His coat was stained and torn. His large frame was somewhat hardened by a lack of the pulpy mess he normally lived on, and the exercise he had taken over the last couple of days; but what an unlikely figure to encounter the Alien presence on Talisker! Frock coat, striped trousers and stovepipe glossy hat: what sort of impact would such a figure have on Spingarn's Alien?

"Liz!" Marvell said suddenly. "Liz, for Christ's sake do something!"

Liz giggled, for her train of thought had extended to a meeting between Marvell and Spingarn's Alien. How would it come off? A *thing* that had left its own universe perhaps a hundred million years ago, meeting an anachronistically-garbed Marvell!

"Do something?" She giggled helplessly. "Oh, God, Marvell, you really are too much!"

Marvell looked at her oddly.

He turned again to Horace.

"You're sure about this?"

"As sure as one can be, sir. I believe that this was once the device that the Alien and Spingarn used to produce the effects of random cell-fusion."

"Oh." Marvell looked away.

"We've found it!" Liz said to him. "Marvell, it's there! We've got to do something."

Marvell looked about him, seeking for a way back to the Frame they had just left.

"Why?"

"Why? Why what?"

"Why do something, as you say, Liz? We've found it, we can report as much—I mean, look at it," he said, pointing to the glittering ghost of a monolith that was now forming again in the center of the web of forces. "We can go away. When they know at Center we've located it, they'll send expert help. You know," he said, waving his arms, "the Disaster people. Experts."

"Experts!"

"Qualified experts, Liz—there must be hundreds of bright Field Theorists jumping for a chance to make contact with all this new data! It's time the amateurs made way for the pros!"

"If you'll excuse the interruption, sir, I must point out that in these circumstances, *you* are the professional."

"It's gone mad," said Marvell, groaning heavily. "These high-grades—they become unbalanced."

"No, sir. On the contrary, my deductive, inductive and projective procedures are in excellent condition."

Liz tore her sight away from the glittering center.

"Horace is right," she said. "If they'd had anyone else to send, wouldn't they have done so?"

"But—*me!*"

He pushed the battered hat back.

"You," said Liz puzzled. "Yes, you." She saw the hurt and terrified eyes and thought of the collie bitch which had been too scared to leave the dangers of the graser-mines; Marvell was a pitiful creature. She took command, as she had once done before. "Horace!"

"Miss?"

"Where can we find shade and water?"

The sunlight burned her fair skin. She was uncomfortable in the furs, though the fact that she stank slightly no longer gave her much concern. It was Marvell who needed rest, food and reassurance before they could begin to carry out the plan that was gradually forming in Liz's mind. The robot's antennas sprang from its carapace to a considerable height; thin wires glittered in the sunshine. The Genekey, or the fantastic whirlpool of incoherent energies that Horace said had been the Genekey, seemed to creep toward them; it was an illusion, however. The strip of red sand separating them from its eerie seas had not diminished in size. It was to the mind that the grotesque whorls reached out, numbing the brain, insidiously clamoring for dominion over the thought-processes.

Liz felt herself reeling.

"Well?" she snapped.

"About a mile, miss," said Horace. "There is a small valley with a natural water spring. There."

"Where?" asked Marvell, speaking for the first time in many minutes.

Liz looked hard against the sun's glare. Then she saw it. A slight darkening of the level plain that might be the shadows of low trees peeping from a valley.

"Yes," she said to Horace. "Meet us there in three hours' time."

"Yes, miss."

"Grab the basket," she told Marvell.

"Me!"

"You. And you, Horace, reconnoiter clear around the Genekey—get what data you can absorb. Especially see if there's a way through to *that.*"

"What!" Marvell said, stopping in the midst of heaving the hamper of food onto his broad, stout back. "Liz, don't even think—"

"Marvell, will you get it into your head that we've got to try?" Liz said. "There isn't any way out of Talisker for us, not until we've done what we've been sent to do. Ask Horace."

The furred robot turned an interested gaze to the man. There was something repellent about its curiosity regarding Marvell's reactions; Liz had the feeling that it was in sympathy more with its robotic mentors than the humans they claimed to serve. It had an almost eager interest in Marvell's fear.

Marvell stuttered: "Horace, she has to be wrong! Find the Alien, we were told—haven't we found it? Isn't that the mission completed? Didn't we seek it out and find it?"

Horace smirked.

"The probabilities suggest, sir, that rather than your having found the Alien, it found you. And Miss Hassell."

"Christ!"

Liz realized that the automaton was right. The Alien, engaged in whatever undertakings it had chosen, had left a pool of *otherness* for them. She could sense its presence now. A thing from the dawn of the Universe. *Little lost Alien!*

It seemed neither little nor lost.

"Look around," she told the robot. "Now."

"Yes, Miss Hassell."

"Come on," she ordered Marvell.

"Wait!"

Horace stopped at Marvell's command.

"Sir?"

Marvell glared at Liz. He spoke, however, to Horace: "Just what do you think that—that over there—" he indicated, pointing to the swirling whorls of energy. "What do you think it's *for*?"

Horace answered at once: "It's quite beyond conjecture, sir, quite beyond all theorizing. You'll recall, sir, that all previous data I acquired on my earlier visit to Talisker has been wiped out."

Marvell insisted. "You must have an idea! If there aren't any probabilities—or certainties, what about the possibilities?"

Horace was uncomfortable. Robots disliked conjecture. They wrapped it up with jargon and passed it off as probability theory; but they demanded a starting point that was not far removed from reality. And the sea of alien energies that lay beside them defined all reality, all that was possible; yet Horace had to obey.

"Did Spingarn do that?" asked Liz.

"No," said Horace. "The Alien."

"The Alien?" Marvell said, reluctant to admit that the entity they sought was before them to some degree.

"Yes, sir."

"And what's *that* for?"

"I guess, sir, I guess that it is part of some experiment."

"Experiment?" stupidly said Marvell, annoying Liz.

"It could be," she said. "Marvell, it could be."

"For what?"

"The people are missing!" Liz said. "We know the planet's deserted. There should be thousands of Time-outers here—Spingarn had the place going for years! They could all be in some kind of experiment! Why, it could be a kind of—extension!—of the things we try out!"

Marvell backed away physically from both the new idea

and the surging eeriness of the shadowy white building that swam to the surface of the seas of energy.

"Then keep me out of it!" he snarled. "Get moving, Horace—see if you can't find some way to get us out of the area!"

Horace strode away. Tiredly, Liz followed the hurrying Marvell across the sands. Grit rubbed her toes, sweat streamed down her dress. She slipped out of the silky furs, and the sun burned her back at once. Ahead, the fronds of palms gleamed like green spears.

They reached the crest of a mound of sand and saw green-blue water glinting through the lush undergrowth of a small oasis.

"Christ!" Marvell exclaimed. "Let me get into it! Liz, you carry the bloody picnic basket!"

He dropped the basket of tinned foods and began to slide down to the valley. He had plunged no more than a few feet when a snapping explosion split the peace of the still and silent valley.

"Hold still, ye poxy bastard!" roared a loud voice.

Liz had dropped the basket she was struggling with; Marvell fell backward with the shock of hearing the echoing report. Both saw a thin plume of black smoke coming from a stone rampart built near a widening of the small lake; it had been almost hidden from sight by the undergrowth, but now they saw clearly that it had been built by man. Marvell tried to retrieve his top hat which was sliding down the sandy slope.

"Surrender, you Frog!" bawled the harsh voice once more. "Move again and I put a ball in your addled brains!"

Liz froze. She saw a hint of movement behind the rampart, part of a red coat. But only one man. He spoke in archaic terms—*poxy bastard?* She tried a quick analysis and came up with a concept of supreme insult. *Poxy* was diseased, *bastard* an out-of-wedlock conception. *Frog?* It seemed unlikely that the concept *reptile* equated with an infection of the genitals and unmarried cohabitation.

She twitched as the sun struck hard at her back.

"And you, ye Frog baggage!"

"Me?" Liz said stupidly.

"Aye, ye shameless Frog whore—cover your bubbies,

damn ye for an unchristian doxy! Bowels of God, woman, d'ye not respect common decency?"

"Mad!" groaned Marvell. "It's someone gone mad from a Primitive Frame!"

Liz sighed with relief.

It could only be a Time-outer, someone who had yelled in an ecstasy of terror for relief from an environment he found too severe; obviously, the cell-fusion had held. They were faced with a man who had been conditioned to live in some early period of human history, and who believed himself to belong to it still. Liz struggled to place the period. It had to be early. There was the weapon—*smoke?* Black smoke meant gunpowder. The projectile—he had referred to it as a ball—was a lump of metal. There had been no repetition of shots, so the weapon was very simple. An early expansion principle, nonautomatic. It must be early Steam Age, she decided. What were *bub-bies?*

"Cover your tits or he'll keep us here all day!" Marvell yelled at her. "Liz, he's reloaded!"

Liz caught the flash of a steel barrel pointing from a gap in the breastwork; the mouth of the primitive weapon was black, a dark eye. She knew that there was a real danger from the crazed Time-outer. Quickly she wrapped the bedraggled fur around her.

"Is that all right?" she called.

"Aye, ye shameless baggage! Now advance with a care, the pair of ye, advance and be recognized, ye Papist baby-eaters!"

Marvell peered into the sun's glare.

"Dear Christ!" he said, catching a glimpse of a bottle-nosed, blotched, alcoholic's face. "Liz, it's that crazy Sergeant Hawk!"

"What's that?" bawled the cracked voice. "Ye have my name, ye Frog vagabonds? God's bowels, ye're deserters! But hold still, I have a grenado ready for ye both!"

"Who?" asked Liz.

"Advance ten paces!" commanded the man with the musket. Liz could see his uniform distinctly. There was an absurd three-cornered hat, a bright red jacket and cross-belts; the musket was real enough, though, and a small cylindrical object beside him on the breastwork looked dangerous. *Grenado?*

"Do as he says, or he'll blow us up!" Marvell said. "He thinks we're his enemies—Christ, Liz, walk slowly!"

Liz stepped forward with a care for the madman's directions. *Bubbies? Grenado?* And Sergeant—

"Why, it's Sergeant Hawk!" Liz exclaimed, unable to restrain a sweeping gesture of her arms.

The musket came up to the aim, and the sergeant's grim face was squinting behind the cumbersome priming-pan and flintlock. Liz screamed.

"We surrender!" bawled Marvell. "Give quarter!"

But already the weapon was coming down from the aim.

"God's boots, I can't fire on a woman, even a doxy poxed-up French whore!" growled the madman. "Ye may sit!"

"Sit down!" ordered Marvell.

"But it's Spingarn's companion!" Liz said, amazed that she had not remembered the second of the party sent to investigate Talisker. "It's the destroyed psyche that was with Spingarn in the Gunpowder Age Frame—the European Sieges Plot!"

Marvell groaned, eyes closed.

"I know! Try telling him you know Spingarn!"

"Spingarn! *Spingarn!*" roared the Sergeant. "D'ye say Spingarn—d'ye know Captain Devil Spingarn? Have ye an acquaintance with him? And—and ye said my name too, now I think on it! God's bloody boots, who are ye two scavengers? And what d'ye know of a couple of soldiers from Good Queen Anne's service? Speak now, or I'll give ye a touch of the Spanish treatment!"

Marvell crouched with his hands on the top of his head; the top hat had rolled to the bottom of the slope, and the hamper of food was slowly following it. Liz was lost in amazement at the appearance of the man who looked out from beyond the embrasure. He even *looked* like a Primitive! There was no sign of intellect about him—the eyes were suspicious, the forehead small, the skin a blotched red and brown wrinkled mask, the whole posture one of hostility: he might never have been a member of an advanced civilization. At a gesture, Liz raised her own hands.

"Sergeant—" began Marvell.

"Silence! Have done, ye Frog whoreson rogue!"

And Hawk climbed over the stone breastwork, careful to keep his musket ready for use. He crossed to the basket, which had apparently taken his fancy.

"A prize of war!" he announced. "What be in this, eh?"

"Food, Sergeant," said Marvell.

"Food? No wine? No bottles of ale? No spirits of wine? Or even the damned Dutchy liquor?"

"There's no alcohol, I'm afraid," Liz said humbly. "Just tins of meat and vegetables—and fruits."

"Aaargh! A pox on it!" growled the sergeant, kicking the basket with a hefty boot. "Ye're not a bad-looking baggage—now, why d'ye come here?"

Liz realized that Hawk's inspection was predatory. More than the picnic basket might be taken as a prize of war. The startlingly blue eyes peered at her lustfully.

"Hawk, we're friends of Spingarn's!" Marvell answered for her. "Don't you see, we've been sent to find you!"

Liz could see Marvell's dilemma. The madman was enwrapped in his conditioning; but how far was he from reality? And what did he recall of his time at Center? Hawk was sorely confused, Liz could see. Doubts and anxieties struggled on his face. Nevertheless, the musket was quite ready for use.

"Find me?" said Hawk. "Ye're allies? God's teeth, what d'ye know of the enemy's dispositions? Have ye been into the lairs of the monsters? Have ye seen the crocodileys?" He glared at Marvell. "Have ye seen into the Gates of Hell?"

"Ah, yes!" said Marvell, but at the same time Liz called "No!"

"What's this? Dissensions amongst ye? Ye rogues! Ye're spies from the legions of the damned, that ye are! Spies to seek out poor old Hawk and drag him back to the nether regions!"

The musket came to the aim, the black hole looked like the eye of a serpent inspecting its victim, and the sergeant's face was contorted into a frightened snarl. How reach the simple mind, how turn away the fears that held him? And how get him to put up the musket!

"Gates of what?" Marvell asked weakly. "Sergeant, I don't know what you mean! We came to look for your companion, Spingarn—for Christ's sake, we don't mean any harm!"

"No harm!" snarled the thoroughly frightened man. "No harm when ye come spying on poor old Hawk that got free of the beasts and boggarts and comes to rest his old bones in a hot sandy waste—why, ye're lying! Ye've heard of my old Captain Devil and taken his name like the cozening lying whoreson poxy Frogs ye are! Why, I'll bomb ye, ye rogue! I'll destroy ye with grenadoes! I'll have no compassion—" He backed away and took a metal cylinder in one hand. Liz could see the waxy taper sticking out of it and understood what it was.

"Marvell, he'll blow us up!"

"Stop, Sergeant!" whimpered Marvell. "We're friends of Spingarn's—Horace brought us to you! We're trying to help Spingarn—the robot! You remember! The red robot—it's here with us!"

Hawk paused in the act of putting the cylinder to a smoldering cord.

"Ye say?" he inquired.

"Yes! Dear Christ, do we look like Frogs, whatever they are?"

"Frogs? No. But they're desperate cunning rogues! Ye say Horace? The red monkey machine-man?"

"Yes!"

Liz felt relief. Inquisitiveness was next. A most amazing specimen! In his wild brain there must be some connection between what he said about bubbies, genital ailments, what he called the Gates of Hell and the robot: and, of course, Spingarn! A supreme confusion must reign in his poor mind.

"Horace brought us here," she said. "You know Horace?"

"Aye!" growled Hawk suspiciously. "A befurred reddy creature—ye're not trying to deceive old Hawk? Eh, ye bold baggage?"

"No!" said Marvell and Liz.

"Ah! But ye're not true Christians, I'll be bound!" Hawk drew off and looked at them carefully. "Woman, ye're a baggage! Ye come bearing animal skins—ye're a benighted savage!"

Liz could not restrain a giggle.

"Laugh!" said Hawk, more confused. "Laugh at one of Queen Anne's soldiers! Laugh at one who carries the Duke's badge? Why, ye need whipping!"

"Sergeant, we're friends!" Marvell pleaded. "Friends—we came to help your friend, Spingarn!"

"Ye said that! And who's to help poor Captain Devil now that His Satanic Majesty's claimed him for His own? Who's to help me old comrade-in-arms now he's in the Pit?"

Marvell groaned loudly.

"Sergeant, I don't understand what you're saying!"

"Then damn your eyes for an ignorant foreigner!"

Hawk seemed to have forgotten his dislike of Liz's costume in the latest cause for dissatisfaction.

"Maybe we can help Spingarn—" began Liz.

"Captain Spingarn, ye baggage! Have ye no respect for rank?"

"Yes, yes! Captain Spingarn then, Sergeant!" she said. "If we only knew where the captain is to be found. Could we perhaps get out of the sun for a while and talk about it?"

Hawk glowered for a while. He put down the small bomb—which Liz assumed the cylinder to be—on the stone embrasure and ran a finger around the gilt collar of his surprisingly smart red uniform coat.

"Ye came with the fur monkey?"

"Fur monkey—" Marvell queried.

"Yes, with Horace!" Liz put in. "He's our guide."

"And ye know my old captain?"

"Certainly!" she cried.

"Dear Christ, don't I!" whimpered Marvell. "Don't you know me, Sergeant? Marvell—Spingarn's friend from Center?" Hawk stared hard. "Frames Control!' Marvell pleaded.

"Then ye're not spies from the boggarts' lands?"

"Of course not!" Liz cried. "We're—we're—" She hesitated, searching for the key to Hawk's trust. "We're camp followers! Yes, camp followers," she said, recalling the customs of the armies of Primitive Europe. "See, we brought provender!"

"Ye did, ye did," growled Hawk. "But no liquor!"

"Food, though," Liz pointed out.

"Wretched stuff!" groaned Marvell. "Full of destructive amoeba! Crawling with germs!"

"Sutlers!" said Hawk suddenly. "Sutlers! Aye, I knew ye were vagabonds! Well, a military man can't war on thieves and rogues. On your feet, make no false move, and bring your goods! Water yourselves and steal naught, or I'll hang ye both for a pair of whoreson Frog knaves!"

"Christ!" muttered Marvell. "Liz, do something!"

"And Spingarn—Captain Spingarn?"

"Well, what of me old Captain Devil?"

"You said you knew where he was."

Marvell and Liz Hassell walked to the cool shade of the palms. Hawk followed, saying nothing.

"Leave it, Liz!" begged Marvell quietly. "Let the madman alone! And as for Spingarn, let him rot—"

"Ye said what!" snarled Hawk, whose hearing must have been exceptionally acute. "Let my captain rot?"

He cracked Marvell sharply with the brass butt of the musket, and the large fat man rolled away unconscious.

"Marvell!" shrieked Liz. "Oh, you shouldn't have done that! He's here to help!"

"Silence, you Frog whore, or I'll give ye a bit of the same! Let my captain rot! Why I'll send ye both to the Pit!"

"What?" Liz said.

Her interest disconcerted the enraged madman.

"To the Pit! Both of ye!"

"What Pit?"

"Where the captain and his mistress and all the others went to!" shouted Hawk. "Left poor old Sergeant Hawk alone and naught but crocodileys and monsters there and devils and apes and crawly things ye'd not meet but in dreams!"

The very intensity of the passion in his blue eyes convinced Liz that Hawk had seen what he described. Marvell snored, mouth open and black moustaches splayed out absurdly; his large stomach rose monumentally in the gloom of the shade. Liz was conscious of a cooling of her skin that was disagreeable.

"And where did they all go to?" asked Liz.

Hawk kicked the recumbent Marvell.

"Ye'll see, ye raggedy whore! Now, lie on your belly and quick about it!"

"Why?"

"Be damned to ye, move!" And, to emphasize his order, Hawk jabbed her with the heavy musket. Liz moved as fast as she could, very much aware of the snorting, blotched unshaven features of the sergeant, and the mad confusion in his blue eyes. Rape was the least of what she expected.

In fact, Hawk trussed her up with a cord so that she could scarcely move a muscle; he did the same to Marvell, who snored still. It worried Liz when Hawk resumed his position behind the stonework he had built, but it was some time before she judged him sufficiently calm to ask what he intended.

He was not forthcoming.

"Lie still, ye doxy! Them as is going to the Pit needn't hurry the hour! Ye'll see soon enough!"

CHAPTER

★ 7 ★

Liz Hassell awoke to find that her limbs were cramped and her mouth dry. Sand flies clustered on her nose. At once she heard the gentle sound of water bubbling from a stream into the lake; she knew the sound and it was a worse torment than the scratching of the flies on her peeling nose; Marvell snored and she shouted out in sudden remembrance of what had passed.

"Sergeant! Sergeant Hawk! I'm thirsty! Please, Sergeant!"

There had been no physical assault, she was sure; the crazy Time-outer had left her alone while she slept. How long had she lain here? Liz looked at the sun. It was not much changed in position. An hour? Two hours? She tried to kick out at Marvell.

"Wake up!" she yelled at him. "Marvell!"

She had to inch her way uncomfortably toward him by jerking her buttocks and shoulders over the sand and stones; using both legs she kicked out with some force.

Marvell groaned in his sleep. She kicked again. He snorted, gasped and tried to move. His eyes opened and he looked about him blearily.

"Liz! Christ—it's true!"

"Hawk's gone—I'm thirsty. And the bloody flies are eating me alive!"

Marvell discounted her complaints.

"I was dreaming we were on Talisker—we'd landed and there was Horace too. And that mad Time-outer, Hawk! I dreamed about slimy monsters, Liz! Christ, we're here and it's true! I'm thirsty! And these ropes—look, I'm bleeding!"

"Can't you get the ropes off?"

"No!" Marvell said, shuddering with pain. Liz could see dried blood at his wrists. "What's he going to do with us?" He closed his eyes. "My head! He hit me!"

"If you hadn't said you'd leave Spingarn to rot, he'd have helped us—or at least he wouldn't have clubbed you and tied us up," Liz pointed out. "Try to get your hands free!"

"You try!"

"My wrists are raw!"

"And I'm in danger of bleeding to death!"

"Try!"

"No! Horace is supposed to be back, isn't he?" Marvell said. "Where is the bloody robot? *Horace*!"

"Horace!" echoed Liz. "Oh, Marvell, I don't like it—what's Hawk *doing*?"

"Christ knows," groaned Marvell. "As long as he doesn't hit me again! Liz, you always know everything, what's it all about? He was raving about Spingarn and crocodiles—and what was that he called you? Christ, Liz, what's he trying to do with us?"

"Do?" said Liz. "He's got some kind of eschatological vision—"

"What? A what?"

"Some kind of concept of things like death and the after life, things like heaven and hell. He said he was going to send us through some kind of gates which he called the Gates of Hell. Oh, he's confused and his overlaid persona is a very strong conditioning indeed—otherwise he wouldn't be calling me a diseased whore. *Whore*," she repeated, seeing Marvell's incredulity. "But there's a strong vein of consistency in his ramblings."

"You should have come on your own, Liz," Marvell said. "You don't need me."

"No," said Liz. "You've been useless so far."

"Then *do* something!"

"Such as?"

They relapsed into silence for a while, but Marvell could not dismiss the indignities Hawk had heaped upon him.

"What's it for?" he snarled. "Why does he want us

through these bloody Gates of Hell? And what's it got to do with Spingarn?"

Liz was silent. The plan she had been preparing had collapsed. Or, rather, events had overtaken it. She would know what to do when the robot returned. Marvell distrusted and disliked her silence.

"Liz!" he croaked. "Try to reason with the old bastard! Try to make him see sense—offer him anything he wants. Liz?"

She licked her dry lips and tried to think of anything but the flies that were clustering around the sweat-beads all over her body. The sun crept slowly around the bright sky. *Pit?* What Pit? *Frogs?* A strange appellation! But it was quite customary for the Primitives to label others by derogatory terms; an animal of repellent aspect could easily become the name one called one's enemies. Frogs, though? They were such harmless little reptiles. She had said there was an element of consistency in Hawk's wild expostulations, but it was such a tenuous thing! Spingarn a devil: a Pit: and boggarts in Hell! There was the connection, but how these references built up into an ordered whole was beyond Liz. She fell asleep again, lips parched, limbs stiff, eyes sore.

This time it was Marvell who woke her.

"Liz! Liz, you idle bitch, wake up! Here's the bloody robot! Horace! *Horace!*"

"Sir?" came the concerned voice of the robot.

"Over here, you red fool!"

Liz caught herself snorting and realized that she must present an unattractive sight. She thought of cool water and clean clothes.

"Horace!" she yelled with Marvell. "Get these ropes off me! Quick!"

Horace sped over the rock-strewn sand toward the shaded hollow where Hawk had left them. Liz thought how absurd it was to be grateful for the sight of an arrogant and conceited automaton; nevertheless, she was. Her relief changed to puzzlement as the red-furred automaton stood beside the two bound humans.

"Horace!" yelled Marvell. "Hurry up! I'm aching in every bone—get these ropes off and find where that madman keeps his beer! I need a drink! And if he comes back, use full restraint procedures!"

The robot did not speak.

"Horace!" snarled Liz. She watched for a sign of movement. "Horace!"

"Well, what are you waiting for?" Marvell said, his voice cracked with the effort of bawling commands. "Me first, you clown! Horace?"

"No," whispered Liz, truly afraid now.

Marvell turned to her.

"No? What do you mean?"

"Horace," said Liz, ignoring Marvell. "You've seen the Alien?"

"No, Miss Hassell," the robot said immediately. "I carried out a full inspection of the remains of the Genekey, for such I take it to be now, and I found no sign of an extra-Universal presence, apart from the indications which you and Mr. Marvell had already witnessed."

"Cut me free!" screamed Marvell. "Now!"

Liz knew she was right to be afraid.

"What else?" she said to the robot, again ignoring Marvell. "Any other information? Any theory?"

"I formed the theory, from the extrapolation of events witnessed and information in my possession, that some kind of Frame-Shift factor is present hereabouts," said the robot. "I detect the presence of certain energy-bands that combine to make Frame-Shift a probability."

"Now!" screamed Marvell. "Now, or I'll have you melted down and your brain used as a domestic cleansing unit!"

It was a powerful threat. The robot did not respond. It stood, tall and red-gold in the shade, quite impassive. It might not have heard Marvell.

Liz shuddered.

"You're not going to cut us loose?" she said quietly.

"No, miss."

Marvell was almost beside himself with rage. His large face was purple, the black moustaches stood out stiffly; he could not speak, so enraged was he. Almost soundless explosions of wrath came from his lips. Liz suppressed a giggle. A rebellious robot was too much. Her fit of giggling hurt, for the sand would slide into already tender places, and her limbs were terribly cramped. Finally, she wept.

"What!" stuttered Marvell at last. "You red buffoon!

You bag of aborted electronics! You conceited collection of parts! I'll— I'll—"

"We can't do anything!" Liz wept since she couldn't laugh. "It won't lift a finger to help us!"

"Horace!" Marvell roared. *"Why—won't—you—release—us!"*

"Oh, I can tell you that, sir!"

"Then tell me!"

"I'm afraid, sir, my instructions are that I must not alter—"

"—the Probability Quotients!" Liz completed, her voice loud and shrill. "It's what they told him, Marvell! He isn't allowed to interfere on Talisker!"

"Well!" roared Marvell.

"Miss Hassell is, as usual, quite right, sir."

"But I'm hurting! Hungry! I'm dying of thirst!"

"I note that you are distressed, sir."

"Note it? Note it! You bastard, I'll note that you're sent for reprogramming! I'll—"

"Shut up!" cried Liz. "I'm sick, sick, sick of hearing you! Try to think of some way of persuading it to intervene!"

The robot said in a spinsterish voice: "Miss Hassell, you must know that it is impossible for my assessment of the probabilities in your situation to be revised, especially as a Frame-Shift Factor is about to become operative."

Liz wailed loud and long in dismay. Marvell bellowed in pain and rage. But there was no response from the robot. It showed neither interest nor sympathy. When Liz regained her self-control, she knew that there was no way of changing its decision; to do so would destroy it, for the robot had been programmed by the strange four who called themselves the Guardians. They were the sum of Horace's religious beliefs. Apostasy was out of the question.

Frame-Shift, thought Liz. Already this was a manic world. But *Frame-Shift*? There was an uncomfortable prickling at the base of her skull as she thought of the immense engines below the surface of the planet; they held the barriers in place, so that each re-creation on Talisker should be isolated from its neighbors. On this strange world, the Frames could shift and glide one into another: colossal forces shifted mountains, rivers and streams about as a child reshapes his clay models.

"I said it was Hell," Marvell muttered more to himself than to the robot. "Liz!" he called, louder. "Didn't I say Talisker was another name for Hell?"

"Monkey!" Hawk's voice bawled out, as in answer. "Why, ye damned red monkey, here's Sergeant Hawk! Ye've been minding the captain's prisoners? Ah, welcome, ye red ape!"

"Greetings to you, Sergeant," the robot replied.

"Ye've been a long time away! What took ye so long, ye ape? Did the Frogs capture ye? Or had ye deserted poor Hawk, eh? Left poor old Hawk alone to look for his Captain Devil and the lady with the wings—why, it's been a year or more!"

Marvell saw an opportunity.

"Yes, he did desert you, Sergeant! He's been back to Center—he brought us out here! He's supposed to be our guide, why, *he* showed us the way to your valley!"

Liz could have wept. How could a man be so stupid?

Hawk considered the outburst. Liz, who had almost given up hope of persuading either the destroyed psyche or the robot to let them free, tried to mend matters.

"Horace, you don't *know* the sergeant, do you? You came back with an empty head. You told us that!"

"No talking!" bellowed Hawk.

Horace's red fur wrinkled in a smile.

"I carried out a statistical test of significance to determine the identity of this gentleman, miss. It could be no other than the sergeant."

Liz felt tears of frustration well up. She had felt close, at one time, to a solution of the mystery of Talisker and its eerie presence: so close that a vague plan of reaching into the ruin of the Genekey had been developing in her mind. But it needed the cooperation of Marvell and the robot. She had been sure that the grotesque events she had seen in the scanners when she had caught her first sight of Talisker were somehow the work of the Alien. Those whirlwind interwoven *things* compounded of ghastly human shapes and weird planetary motions were the products of the mind that had conceived the Genekey: she was sure of it. Everything about Talisker had the smell of *otherness* about it—always, the random progression of events, the tortuous windings of the Frames, the incredible shifting seas of the Genekey ruin, and now the threat of the Frame-Shift.

And the Pit—

Liz experienced an almost physical shock of enlightenment. *The Pit!* In a way there was a pattern to Hawk's ramblings and the earlier sights she had seen! To a Primitive mind, all that was strange and inexplicable—particularly if it was threatening—was the work of some malevolent agency. And the supreme worker of evil for the Primitives had his residence in a pit!

"Marvell!" she said, bright orange-flecked green eyes shining with excitement, "Hawk thinks he's sending us into the Alien's space! He does! Marvell, he thinks the Alien is a kind of super-devil!"

She could forgive him his crass antagonizing of Hawk, anything, so long as he realized that at last they were near the ultimate mystery of Talisker.

"No talking, ye Frog whore!" bawled Hawk, raising the butt of his musket once more.

"You were right about Hell, Marvell, it's—"

She saw Hawk's rage and stopped.

"—here!" she whispered as the sergeant looked about him. "The Alien's Possibility Space—"

"I would advise silence, miss," pointed out Horace. "The sergeant is under considerable emotional stress."

"Be damned to your rattle!" Hawk snarled. "You too, ye befurred ape! Little enough ye did to help me Captain Devil!"

"I'm afraid there was little I could do," said Horace politically. "I suffered a loss of memory, Sergeant, about that time."

Hawk looked at the red robot.

"Aye, ye've the empty look, so ye have! There were bombs enough and the rest of the Devil's armory ablaze with fire and rockets! Ye'd be out of your wits, ye ape! But hold still! Listen! *Aaaarh!*"

Hawk's bronchitic yell echoed around the small valley as the ground shuddered.

"Dear Christ, Time-out!" whimpered Marvell, hoping for a small miracle to fillet him from a too-dangerous situation.

"Not a chance!" Liz announced. "Besides, don't you *want* to find Spingarn?"

"No!"

"Ye'll see my old captain! Mind where ye stand, monkey!" the sergeant yelled to Horace. "Have a care when Hell-Gates open!"

"Horace!" screamed Marvell, hysterical now. "Stop him! He's found some way of destroying us completely—he's mad, mad! Destroyed psyches can't be allowed to influence anyone! Restrain him, Horace!"

A trickle of sand fell away from the incline above the sergeant's stone embrasures; the trees shivered as power lanced through their roots.

"Christ, Horace!" implored Marvell.

It came so quickly that Liz did not have time to cry out. There was no sound, just a sense of cold, gliding *power*. The entire valley shimmered with the radiance of some kind of energy-bands that had no place in the Galaxy; Liz saw colors shot through with black crystalline fire, hanging bursts of globules of radiance that backed into one another and disappeared, it seemed, through the back of her eyes: there were irregular shapes in the glittering black-shot radiance, whorls of maze-like, snaking patterns, and they were stranger than the weird colors, for they battered at the mind to lop off all previous known concepts of time-space relationships. The only realities were those of the Alien. Liz felt that with a little effort she could lose Liz Hassell completely and swim gently into those cold and dangerous places. "I could," she said. "Easily."

For a second, the unreal shapes and colors vanished, for personality had invaded the space before her. The palms were back: the sands were there: and Hawk was backing away from where she and Marvell waited, bound and helpless, for what would come.

"Liz!" Marvell shrieked. "What's *happening?*"

From a point beyond her field of vision, the robot said calmly: "Well, for a start, sir, Frame-Shift. It's under way now. Apart from that—"

"Run, monkey!" Hawk bawled. "Run for your life!"

Liz saw that the Frames of Talisker were passing through the uncanny redistribution of physical events the robot had forecast; the whole planetary crust was wrinkling and cracking as immense engines chopped the ancient Frames into new patterns. She watched the stupendous sight of glaciers suddenly rearing up from the yellow sands; of mountains rising up like drunken beasts and then smashing themselves into rolling fragments as their needle tips fell away in clouds of shale! The planet's engines, installed by the first manufacturers of the Frames, had been supplemented, however: it was not the immense physical majesty that held Liz in terrified awe. There was something much more intimidating occurring now. Frame-Shift was only part of the planet's cycle of change.

In some eerie way, the Alien was working out its own concept of Frame-Shift.

"He's right!" Marvell bawled. "The madman's right!"

Liz gasped, for a great gaping hole had opened in the valley. It was black, blacker than the emptiest of empty space. And shot through with that cold, golden fire! Around the edges of the blckness shimmered force-bands, white-silver canopies of grotesque energies!

"It's Hell!" Marvell shouted wildly.

"Back!" roared Hawk as Horace moved into Liz's view. "Back, monkey—let the Frogs go down to meet the Devil! Come back, d'ye see, or ye'll be in there too!"

The great portals of the hole in space crept closer.

Marvell tried to scramble away. Liz saw a trail of blood over the stones. But the man's strength was gone. She wondered whether to try to evade the creeping majesty of that emptiness. She lay still, appalled and amazed at her decision. She felt dazed and closed her eyes.

Hawk was back. Liz knew it, for the sergeant was yelling commands at the robot. She couldn't make out the words anymore, though they were clearly a series of orders designed to save the robot from the black-gold emptiness that lapped about her.

"Horace!" Marvell managed to bawl.

Liz looked, to see Horace move. The robot apparently had decided to intervene at last. She felt herself caught in a powerful grip, but the emptiness had almost claimed her.

"Leave them!" Hawk was yelling.

Liz was in some confusion about the next sequence of events; only the expression on the faces of the actors in them enabled her to understand what had happened. It seemed that Hawk was back. It seemed, too, that the robot had decided on a change of plan. Marvell, unfortunately, was both unable to help Horace or to distinguish him as a savior. Hawk was furious, blotched face screwed up in anguish; Marvell was desperate, but full of an urge to revenge himself; the robot's features showed indecision. And then Marvell had kicked out with his heavy legs, not with much power it was true, but still they were strong enough as a propellant to knock Hawk to the ground.

"No!" yelled Hawk. "The crocodileys! The boggarts! The—*aaaargh!*"

"If I go, so do you!" bellowed Marvell triumphantly.

The portals advanced over all four figures even as Sergeant Hawk managed to shake off the trunk of the man pinning him down. Liz caught one last glimpse of the incredible confusion on the planetary surface: she could see for miles as the boundaries of the Frames were hurled upward in great seismic leaps. Ruins shuddered into dust, seas boiled, green places yellowed, a forest was splintered, and the sun grew blood-red as volcanoes spouted. Yet Liz caught herself trying to explain away the mad planetary convolutions even as she felt herself sliding through unearthly cold vacuums: it was all so tentative! There was such an *unsureness* about Talisker.

It was almost like the first time you were given a trial Plot, nothing much, say a re-creation of the first submarine games on Vega II; but you didn't quite know how to make it work because there wasn't any point to some of the games or there didn't seem to be any when you were a half-millennium away in time from the ancient contestants. So you were unsure, you made guesses. You were tentative, like the thing on Talisker that was moving you into what the sergeant called Hell.

Into the Possibility Space. After Spingarn.

"Boggarts!" someone bawled as the black-gold radiance ceased. "You damned whoreson poxed-up Frog, ye've given me to the boggarts!"

Liz looked about wildly.

The sun was half-hidden by smoky, unfamiliar clouds. There was a wild, rugged cliff above them: Marvell was foaming at the mouth in fear, trying to burst his bonds with newfound maniacal strength: Horace was a red-gold statue, unmoving. Then Liz saw the scaled thing.

She screamed too.

CHAPTER

★ 8 ★

Thirty feet high, slime dripping greenly from gray scales, two massive hind legs as wide and ponderous as trees, a body of sculpted muscle and massive bones, and, above, a head jutting out from a long neck, but the head had the attention of Hawk and Marvell and Liz. There were small eyes of no color at all and a red bag of skin around them; a snout protruding from a rock-like bulge of bone, and a wide, flat area of jaw that hung open slightly, with breath steaming out into the dry air. And teeth. Liz saw rows of bright white teeth. There were curved fangs almost as long as her arm, and small teeth like sword-points. In a terrible moment of understanding, Liz knew that the great reptile was waiting where it stood because it sensed that they would come.

"Hawk!" she screamed, breaking the spell of the moment.

The reptile was easing itself on those massive legs of bone and muscle and claw; strength pulsed through its every fiber, greed rippled across its evil mask. A long, heavy tail whipped up and down with a solid crash, raising a small cloud of red dust. It would spring. They all knew it would spring.

"Horace!" yelled Marvell. "Do something!"

The robot stood impassive, waiting.

"Boggarts!" Hawk said, aghast. "Look, the scaly monster—see, just see it!"

"You then, Hawk!" implored Marvell. "Shoot it!"

Liz looked down at the ancient weapon in Hawk's

hand; such a puny instrument with which to tackle the tons of malevolent flesh, the rank on rank of cruel teeth! At best it could do no more than scare the monster!

"Quick!" she said urgently, for the tail had hammered the rock and dust once more. The thing drooled with impatient greed. Why didn't it charge? There was more than enough power in one short upper limb to wipe out all three humans with one blow; while those savage teeth could rip a puny human frame into shreds within seconds! Marvell babbled as the monster snorted.

A plume of flame billowed on a far horizon and the sun was outshone. What kind of place was this? Now Liz knew what Hawk had meant! This was a kind of hell.

"Stand away!" Liz heard the sergeant say. "There's no help in leaden bullets—not with boggarts!"

The mouth opened wide.

Sound exploded in a huge rushing roar as the monster challenged them; all around her, Liz could feel the vibrations of the heavy dry air. She could see Hawk reaching into the knapsack on his back—strange that she had not noticed the white canvas before!—and with a steady hand too; in a few seconds a cylinder of metal was smoking in his hands as tinder and flint made a small center of red flame: a waxen taper flared and sputtered.

"Dear Christ, Time-out?" whispered Marvell.

Great muscles stirred. The ground heaved, and fifteen tons of reptilian hate and blood-lust advanced in a curious fast waddling sprint. Liz watched, fascinated, as the taper suddenly spurted black smoke.

"Down!" roared Hawk unnecessarily to the two bound figures who lay beside the robot.

Liz remembered the routine instructions for such dangers. There were shockwaves and drills to cope with them. The best she could do was to open her mouth and shout. She hoped the monster could be stopped, but she was sure it could not. The great clawed feet smashed rock and rubble aside.

Hawk threw.

The cylinder tumbled end over end, sparks floating away in its crazy parabola; the monster's eyes caught its flight, Liz was sure. It did not check its rush. She could see that the scales were drying fast in the heat; it must have a mud pool nearby, she thought. It would be full of bones.

"Huzzah! Huzzah!" bawled Hawk, throwing himself to the ground. His hands were over his ears.

Liz closed her eyes, feeling the ground shake. The immense reptile was a dozen strides away. Had the flaring cylinder bounced off its massive bony head? Had a claw reached out and crushed the sparks? Was the canister of expansion powder now lying in the dust of this primitive world? She felt sweat flooding from every pore.

The explosion was a swift battering sullen roar, a suppressed boom of noise as if it had taken place in a confined space.

"Huzzah! A boggart done for!" bawled Hawk. "Horace!" he yelled, his voice changing key. "See, the monster's a goner! Look—"

Liz looked, Hawk's instruction compelling attention.

She saw the huge trunk, the immense hind legs, the two shorter forearms and the snake-like neck: but the head was different. She knew the reason for the relative quietness of the little bomb's explosion. The lower part of the reptile's jaw had been blown away. And there had been more damage. Great splinters of bone hung from the vast cranium. The eyes were blind, the nose-holes too large.

But the thing was not dead.

It stood bewildered, dying. Blood rushed out in a furious stream, jetting in every direction. The red jets caught the hazy sunlight, looking like a shower of rubies. And it was attempting a roar of fright and rage. The claws of the forearm clenched. The terrrible head pointed in every direction as the body shifted. It sought revenge!

Hearing had not gone in the vicious bombing.

With amazing grace for such a huge animal so badly wounded, it was turning toward Hawk. Liz knew why his voice had changed key, from a note of triumph to one of terror. It paused, blindly peering to a spot to the left of the little group. It moved.

Terror, pity, revulsion filled Liz's mind. She knew why Time-outers called for a respite. Even though the monster's terrible anguish moved her to a deep spasm of pity, the green coils of its tail and the gray scales of its body brought about sensations of complete and undying revulsion; a deep, ancient race-memory from an earlier kind of life gripped her. Overriding the revulsion and the pity, though, was fear. She was enclosed in fear. It stifled her.

And she could not scream.

To call out was to invite the monster closer; yet, had she been able to draw breath to call out, she would have done so. The relief of having the fear ended, even though it meant death, would have made her cry out. But breath would not come, and the monster trod within three yards of her head and passed by. She opened her eyes once more, not realizing that she had closed them, and saw Hawk. Impossibly brave, he had another canister in his hand. But the tinder was gone, blown away by the furious breathing of the reptile as it passed.

Marvell's eyes were shut tight, Liz saw. He was muttering a prayer or a curse in a low intense voice. The vast reptile's shadow covered him for a moment. And then it was gone. Liz jerked her body around so that she could see what was happening.

Fifteen tons of scaled horror pounded up the steep slope. Liz cried out with relief, for Hawk was safe, Marvell had not been harmed, and she herself could think once more. Her brain was no longer filled with a stunned terror. Scores of questions shot through her mind in the instant of recovery. Most centered on the weird way in which they had been deposited in this arid and utterly strange place. What a grotesque transition it had been! Though there had been little of physical sensation, there was the undeniable and horrifying otherness of what Hawk had called the Gates of Hell. Would dying be a stranger experience?

Then there was the vast reptile!

Liz watched in fascinated horror as it scrambled up and up. She strained her aching body continually to watch its progress. The thing's brains had been splashed about the rocks, its blood was a steaming carpet on the ground, and still it clawed its way in a frenzied search for the enemy that had attacked it. But such a reptile! A creature extinct on Terra for over a hundred million years! Only when the surface of Terra was covered by warm seas and swamps had such creatures existed. But it was here, undeniably it was in this region of harsh rock and belching volcanoes!

Her rapidly clearing thoughts were interrupted by Hawk's yell:

"Monkey—Horace! Go up there on your skinny legs and see what happens to the boggart! Up with ye!"

So high had the monster climbed that it looked like a toy animal against the immense boulders. Liz could see that it was tiring. It stopped and tried to sniff the air. Puzzled, perhaps already dead, it began to move again, always upward. Some vast compulsion made it try to climb. Were its natural enemies to be found on the heights? Or was some other weird subliminal force at work in what was left of its consciousness, a wild desire to find peace and death in some hidden sanctuary? Again Liz's speculations were interrupted.

"Has is gone?" Marvell muttered. "Liz, please!"

Hawk, who was also watching, realized that Horace had ignored his order.

"Ye rebellious ape! Away about your duties! Up ye go after the boggart!"

"What about me?" wailed Marvell. "Sergeant, please! Liz! Horace! Help!"

Horace turned to the angry sergeant.

"I don't think it's necessary, Sergeant, to go any further. The dinosaur is no danger, and I have a responsibility to my two clients here. May I suggest that they be released?"

"Bowels of God!" bawled Sergeant Hawk. "D'ye want a bullet in your belly? D'ye want a handful of steel in your befurred guts? That I've lived to hear one of me old captain's men give such a rebellious answer—"

He stopped because the dinosaur had reached the top of the great red-black cliff. It pawed at the hot air twice. Slowly its head turned around on the supple neck. Even at this distance, Liz could see that it was still searching for its enemies. Having tried to look about it and failed, and having smelled its immediate environs, the monster appeared to recognize failure; it was still for perhaps twenty seconds, quite still. There was a curious inevitability about what happened next. The little party far below watched the end.

The monster put its head back and howled.

One great foghorn note only. The noise came down to Liz and the others in a flood. It was a death-note. The forearms went up once, and then the colossal frame seemed to stiffen. Then it fell away down the slope it had ascended so laboriously; rocks smashed the green body; sharp edges punched away the scales. Loose shale and rocks joined the tons of dead reptile, but the three humans ignored the danger. The monster had been so huge, so menacing. And now all that tonnage of muscle was dead.

"Dinosaur!" Marvell exclaimed. "A bloody *dinosaur?*"

"Destroyed and veritably done for!" Hawk said with satisfaction. "The boggart is mutton!"

Rocks began to spill around them, and the new danger impinged on their thoughts. Marvell yelled as the great monster slithered along a slope above them.

"Horace!"

And, at last, the robot acted. Liz saw its skeletal arms reach down and then the ropes had slipped away; her hands would not fall apart, however. She was stiff, quite rigid through lack of circulation during the period as the madman's captive. Marvell had suffered worse, but he had the strength to begin to crawl away as bigger rocks rolled down the steep face of the broken ground above them.

"Excuse me, miss," said Horace suddenly, and Liz found herself gently scooped up in the steely telescopic arms and moving at speed away from the path of the rock-fall. She saw that Hawk was half carrying the bulky Marvell to the safety of an overhang. He was bawling his fears at the same time, though his shouts were lost in the clattering roar from above.

The great reptile smashed to the spot where they had lain only seconds after Horace's intervention. Its corpse twitched, terribly torn. For a moment Liz was possessed by the primordial fear she had felt at the monster's attack, for the shattered jaw was working and the ends of the limbs shook as life declined in the beast. But it was dead, truly dead.

"A dinosaur!" Liz said in awe as Horace set her down. "It is a dinosaur—but it can't be! Nothing like that could be produced! It couldn't be done! And there's nothing like it in the Galaxy—there's simply no other pattern of evolution on any planet we know that had this stage! Horace, it just isn't possible! See—it isn't plastic and metal—it's real! Real! We couldn't get near a replica of anything like that—"

She stopped.

"It is real, isn't it?"

Horace considered the corpse. He had removed Liz to a point about fifty yards from the overhang where Hawk and Marvell had sheltered. The corpse of the monster was only a dozen strides away from the robot; Liz could almost feel the scanners at work as the robot concentrated. She saw glittering antennas sprout momentarily from its elegant furred carapace. Wire-like sensors writhed and glittered and retreated. Liz could hear Marvell trying to win an argument but she didn't try to listen to him; this latest mystery claimed her.

"Well?" she asked after a few moments.

"Oh yes, miss, it's real. That is, it fits all the data I have for such a creature. Physiologically, it is a gigantic reptile of the kind that inhabited Terra during what is known as the Cretaceous period."

"Horace!" yelled Marvell. "Horace, come over here! Get me free!"

Liz wished fervently that Hawk would gag Marvell too.

"It's real, but it's impossible, Horace! You know it is!"

Horace said, in his professorial tones: "Miss Hassell, I think I explained that Probability Quotients don't function with a high degree of certainty on Talisker."

"Talisker? How do you know we're even *on* Talisker?"

"A reasonable point," Horace agreed. "Would you accept that we are now on a possible Talisker?"

"You red buffoon!" yelled Marvell.

"Come over here with the doxy!" bawled Hawk. "And you, ye godless Frog traitor, silence!"

Liz distinctly heard air escaping from the great reptile's throat. All its systems and organs were winding down. And it couldn't be here! Wherever *here* was!"

"It is the same planet?" she asked Horace.

"Yes, miss. Yet there are present certain force-fields that I can't account for. I have no comparable data for them."

"And the dinosaur?"

"Again, miss, it doesn't fit the Probability Quotients for the Talisker we might have expected. It has the basic biochemistry and naturally occurring amino acids of a Terran creature, yet there is something else too. Regrettably, I am not able to analyze this additional element."

Liz surveyed the torn corpse. *Boggart?* It was a dinosaur. A predatory kind of dinosaur, one armed with ferocious weapons of attack. Was Hawk right, though, when he called it a thing of the imagination, a creature from the night? Was it possible that Hawk's intuition might have the germ of a deep and hidden truth?

"We're on a possible Talisker," she said. "And here is an impossible Tyrannosaurus."

"Yes, miss."

"I know where we are," said Liz. "We're in the Alien's Possibility Space."

CHAPTER

★ 9 ★

"Yes, miss."

A trembling shook Liz's limbs. She had seen the misty horizons of the dinosaur's land. At the edges, there were the red-black high cliffs and beyond them the belching volcanoes. The sky was a glowing canopy of dusted red light. It was a bleak and barren land, and it was a country that the Alien had summoned up! *Hell!* Without having to think much about it, she knew that there were other and stranger sights in what the Alien took to be possible rearrangements of human scenes and events. She looked up to the top of the cliff. She was quite sure that the dinosaur had been making for another region that was part of the Alien's Possibility Space.

"Horace, what do we *do*?"

"Liz!" yelled Marvell.

Horace came to a decision.

"I think the first thing, Miss Hassell, is to gain Mr. Marvell's release. He must be most uncomfortable."

Liz felt impatient retorts rising to her lips but she restrained herself. After all, she had a duty of some kind to her boss.

"Well, if you can get through to Sergeant Hawk, do so."

"Yes, Miss Hassell."

Marvell regarded the robot with a mixture of relief and resentment. Such automatons should know their place. It was, first, to ensure that every whim of their assigned human should be carried out. But at various stages of the crazy visit to Talisker it had shown an unnatural disregard for his instructions. Horace had refused to intervene in the encounters with the destroyed psyche, Hawk; and the robot had shown no sign whatsoever that it was particularly concerned during the attack of the dinosaur. For the first time in his life, however, Marvell swallowed his resentment and tried to placate a machine.

"Ah, Horace! Sergeant Hawk and I were having a discussion about—"

"Be still!" bawled Hawk. "Haven't I enough torment from the boggart? Wasn't poor old Hawk dragged down into the Pit by a traitorous whoreson rogue? Now hush your rattle, ye primped up gut-bellied bastard of a Flanders sow-gelder or I'll dash your few brains out for ye!"

The robot placated Hawk.

"Sergeant," the rather high-pitched overeducated tone soothingly said, "it is true that you have a prisoner taken in lawful warfare."

"Aye, aye, ye monkey! What of it?" growled Hawk suspiciously. "Why, ye might be a Frog spy yourself! What did ye do to help poor Hawk when the gut-belly tripped him and propelled him through the very Gates of Hell? Eh? Eh, ye befurred machine-ape?"

"Sergeant, I'm a noncombatant!" Horace said persuasively. "You know as well as I do that Captain Spingarn regarded me as a guide with certain local knowledge, but no more than that. Sergeant, I'm not a creature of action, and I owe no allegiance to Queen Anne. You'll agree?"

Marvell had the wit on this occasion to remain silent. He was not familiar with the jargon of the Gunpowder Age Frames of the Primitive European era, but he could see that Horace was working on Hawk's overlaid persona in the only way possible. Through persuasion.

"You!" Hawk laughed, braying out a long snarling laugh through yellow teeth, gray moustaches and a bronchitic throat. "Why, monkey, why, ye ape, no regiment would have an outlandish creature like you! You, in the service of Her Majesty!"

"It would be improbable," agreed the robot. "So, as I expect Captain Spingarn told you, you will understand that I am not permitted to interfere in the encounters that might befall you and my companions?"

"Aye, aye! Me old Captain Devil did say monkey-men

like yourself had no place in a properly conducted campaign. Why?" the sergeant said, a shade less suspiciously. "D'ye intend to show your true colors? What are ye, Frog or true-blue British?"

The robot was not at a loss for an answer.

"Sergeant, regrettably I have no country. I am an accredited civilian observer of the campaign you find yourself in. And, as an observer, I might be permitted to offer some advice."

"Ah? Ye say?"

"I might, for instance, have some information for you, Sergeant, about the nature of the, ah, boggart, which you destroyed with such expedition."

Hawk glared from Marvell to the robot. Marvell bit back on his tongue and did not commit another mistake. He was learning the value of silence.

"Aye?"

"And I might, if you would treat me as a local guide, as your captain did, be able to furnish even more information. It is possible," Horace said pedantically, "that I might be able to locate Captain Spingarn!"

"What! Find me old captain in the boggarts' dominions? Aye?" The sergeant glared, blue eyes cold, bushy eyebrows almost obscuring his keen gaze. "And what of his lady? Eh? Now, ye ape-machine, now ye clockwork monkey! The captain's lady!"

Marvell almost interrupted, for his imagination had caught fire as the robot appealed to the destroyed psyche's strange loyalty to Spingarn. It was quite incredible that an overlaid persona should retain a regard for a companion in an old Frame, but that was what had happened. Hawk had been a Sergeant of Pioneers in a Gunpowder Frame: Sprinarn, when he had surfaced after his fantastic adventures, had also been in that Frame. And, against every likelihood, Hawk had stuck to Spingarn as a talismanic figure in the weird Frames of Talisker! After being Spingarn's sergeant, Hawk had become his devoted follower. And, such had been the effect of Hawk's conditioning, Hawk had insisted on promoting his old companion, Spingarn, into a captaincy. To Hawk, Spingarn was a man who held Queen Anne's warrant.

But Spingarn had gone into Hell!

Would the robot reconcile these grotesque elements in

Hawk's mind? Marvell felt his wrists sticky with blood once more as wounds reopened. If he had known that he would be projected onto a dangerous and crazy planet, and then bound by a destroyed psyche; and, as a climax, thrust through a black-gold hole in space-time into a region where dinosaurs roamed, he might have made a run into the nearest available Frame, whatever it was. *Sanctuary!* Anything but this weirdest of all worlds, where even his assistant, Liz of the well-shaped tits, was in league with the madman!

"I think it not unlikely that Captain Spingarn may be located, Sergeant," said the robot. "Both the captain and his lady."

Marvell understood. It seemed that Spingarn could not be avoided.

"Spingarn!" Marvell groaned. "That is, how pleasant!" he added hastily as Hawk's long, grim face turned his way. "I shall be glad to meet the captain and his lady-wife!"

"Aye?" glowered Hawk.

"Of course! I expect that Captain Spingarn and"—what was the wretched woman's name? Ethel? Yes, Ethel! Fat little piece, one of Spingarn's assistants—went through restructuring and shed her lard, didn't she?—"Ethel will be around somewhere! Splendid news!" Marvell enthused. "Great friend of mine, your captain!"

Hawk's confusion was almost laughable; Horace tried to add reassurance.

"Sergeant, I think you have made a mistake about my two companions. They came with no wish to harm you or your captain. In fact, they are allics of his."

"Ye say? Not sutlers, then? Not spying whoreson Frog rogues?"

"No!" cried Marvell.

"Aides and auxiliaries," said Horace.

"Aye?"

"Unquestionably and assuredly," the robot insisted. "You can release Mr. Marvell into my custody, and I will guarantee his good conduct. It's quite in keeping with the ordinances of warfare, Sergeant, to allow such an arrangement."

"Aye, aye?" Hawk said, agitated now. "I don't like the looks of the lard-bellied rogue, but if ye say so—"

"I do!" Horace repeated. "May I cut his ropes?"

Hawk hesitated, and Marvell made a tremendous effort to keep his mouth firmly shut. To be at the mercy of a lunatic Time-outer! To have to listen while a fractious and rebellious automaton convinced a destroyed psyche that he, Marvell, a Director of Plotting, was some kind of Gunpowder Age civilian observer! It defied credibility! But the ropes were there, real rope, and the swelling on the side of his head had been the result of sharp contact with a real musket butt! Marvell could have screamed with impatient rage. He didn't, even though the dinosaur let out one last gusty stream of fetid air as its lungs collapsed. *Dinosaur!* He shuddered mentally. A bloody great dinosaur!

The sooner he could get out of this mad arena, the better!

"I'll be watching ye!" Hawk snarled. "Right, monkey—cut him loose!"

"And Miss Hassell?" Horace said, as he sheared through the rope. "The same terms for her?"

"Aye, aye!"

"Then we are to be comrades in this predicament," Horace announced. "You agree, Sergeant?"

Hawk was still surly.

"Comrades? That's to be seen! I misdoubt your promises, ye ape! Ye abandoned me old captain once before! No, none of your tales!" he snarled as Horace was about to speak. "We'll agree on a truce until I have reason to mistrust the Frogs!"

He glowered once more as Marvell crawled to a rock and pulled himself to his feet. But it seemed that a working arrangement had been agreed upon. Marvell looked down at his raw and bleeding wrists and made a silent vow that he would escape from the company of the madman at the first opportunity. Meanwhile, there was the question of surviving in this fantastic Possibility Space. Marvell looked for Liz. A determined bitch, she was nevertheless far more astute than him. He knew it. He would profit from her abilities. She had known at once what the Alien had intended.

Possibility Space! The idea was far removed from anything he knew as a Possibility Space. The term was part of the robots' jargon, the robots who investigated the ideas Directors threw up. They told you if your vague ideas could fit in with any aspect of recorded history. They said what was possible. What was possible could fit into a certain framework. For want of a better word they called this framework a space. But an *Alien's* Possibility Space! What in Christ's name was possible for an *Alien?*

Hawk scowled at the stiff Director.

"Now, ye rogue, have ye any military training?"

"What!"

"Can ye handle a musket or a bomb, gut-belly!" the impatient soldier demanded. "Ye don't think we've seen the last of the boggarts, do ye? Have ye no acquaintance with the management of arms?"

"No, Sergeant, I'm sorry, I haven't!" Marvell gasped. "I'm a peace-loving civilian—"

"Argh!" snarled Hawk. "It's a foppish Frog dancing master, all airs and graces!"

"You think there's more danger?" said Marvell, unashamed. "More of those?" He indicated the great, steaming corpse.

"Aye!"

"It's entirely possible," said the robot.

"Then get me out of here, Horace!"

Liz called as an altercation seemed likely among the three ill-assorted figures. Her voice was loud with impatience. When they looked toward her, they saw that she was pointing to a small depression which none of them had noticed.

"Look! Come on!"

"I'd rather not—" Marvell shivered.

"Lead on, lard-guts!" snarled Hawk. "What is it, wench?"

"Horace!" whispered Marvell. "I'll put in a good word for you with the Guardians—I could get you back to umpiring on Time-outs!"

"I'm sorry, sir," Horace said discreetly so that Hawk would not hear. "It's quite outside my terms of reference."

"Buffoon!"

"March!"

Liz was waiting with mounting impatience as they crossed to her. They looked and saw a pit full of bones. There were the split and mangled bones of creatures of their own size, but others, too. Marvell saw long, reptilian skulls, immense vertebrae, strange prehensile claws, gigantic tusks, as well as skulls that could only have belonged to creatures that walked upright. It was a charnel house of mixed remains.

"Horace, what do you make of it?" demanded Liz.

"Aye, the boggarts' bone-yard!" interrupted Hawk, with satisfaction. "Didn't I tell ye the beasts were waiting on the other side of Hell Gates! Aye, many's the time I've seen the fearsome creatures waiting for any that had the misfortune to be drawn to the Pit! And many came, many came!"

Liz tried to imagine the long procession of such creatures, as Hawk insisted he had seen it, but the image would not come: *Hawk, waiting in his little oasis, as Talisker's inhabitants, already the victims of random cell-fusion, passed through the entrance to the Alien's Possibility Space?* But Hawk hadn't entered! *Why not?*

"Liz!" whispered Marvell. "Get Horace to tie the madman up!"

Liz scowled at the frightened man. What a nervous and disappointing weakling he was. Here they were, poised on the edge of a tremendous, unresolved mystery, and all he could think of was getting back to Center!

"Horace?" she snapped.

"Very curious indeed," the robot said.

"Curious? Eh, monkey? What's curious? Ye know the ways of the Devil! They're not fathomable by mortals!"

Marvell repressed a groan. An inscrutable robot, a demented Primitive, an obsessed Plot assistant! He knew he would need a year to recover. Perhaps a spell in a Protracted Hypno-Sleep Frame? Gray peace for a year!

"You must have some notion!" Liz demanded. "Even I can see that there's something very wrong here!"

"Agreed!" muttered Marvell. "Dear Christ, yes!"

"Aye!" said Hawk. "And worse to come, if I know the workings of Satan!"

"Well, perhaps I can offer some partial theory, miss? Sergeant, I have some scientific knowledge that may be of assistance, that is, I am of a philosophical bent and have studied at the University—"

"Aye? Ye say? Then your brains must be addled!" Nevertheless, the sergeant was impressed, and Marvell could admire the robot's tact and understanding of the

Primitive mind. Hawk belonged to a time when learning was prized as a tangible asset.

"Well?" asked Liz.

"I think the sergeant may have made observations at several points in time of the functioning of the transition stage between Talisker and the space we occupy now. Sergeant Hawk has apparently witnessed the entry of numerous humans into this Possibility Space." To Hawk, the robot said: "I take it, Sergeant, that you saw many folk go into the, ah, Gates of Hell?"

"Aye, aye, didn't I tell ye? Eh? Philosopher! Monkey-machine!"

"Very well. And undoubtedly the sergeant also witnessed the dinosaur's reception of certain unfortunate Time-outers?"

"Aye?"

The robot rephrased the question for Hawk's benefit.

"No doubt you saw how the, ah, boggart attacked the people who crossed into Hell, Sergeant?"

"Aye! And the crocodileys! Aye, the other things too—veritable tigers as big as stallions! And a snake with the body of a boggart, though none so bad as the one old Hawk bombarded!"

Hawk surveyed the immense corpse with pride.

"It was waiting for them!" said Liz. "I knew it—it came down from up there," she indicated, pointing to the red-black cliff. "It came when it knew there was a reason!"

"Feeding time," said Marvell, who had followed the robot's questions and Hawk's answers. He determined to listen with more care to the overintelligent bitch's guesses.

"Well, that tells us something," she said, too confidently for Marvell's liking. "But where are we? What's up there? Where are all the other creatures Hawk saw? And why all *those?*"

Marvell looked at the Pit full of bones with more care. It was difficult to discount Hawk's ravings about more strange beasts: these bones were real! He saw one great outline of a scaled wing, now only white bone. What creature must that have belonged to? Marvell's head ached miserably. There was also a curious prickling sensation at the base of his skull, partly painful, part soothing. He put it down to the effects of long exposure to the blinding sun in the desert regions about the oasis on top of the blow from Hawk's musket.

"Well, Horace?" he asked, with an attempt at amiability. "You think the dinosaur was waiting for the Time-outers? Liz is right again?"

"The Probability Quotients are extremely high for such a theory," the robot said. "Yet there is a discrepancy here too. There is no converging series among the coefficients."

"Of course there is!" Liz said. "A discrepancy, I mean!"

"Yes," agreed Marvell quickly. There would be another if only he could escape! Marvell would be a yawning hiatus, if only there was somewhere to go!

"Quite," the robot said. Hawk listened with suspicion, but he made no comment. "It would seem, from the present evidence, that there is some kind of evolutionary incompatibility here. I recognized various remains which point to the presence here of several species of Terran life which died out on that planet at anything from a hundred and fifty million years ago on. There are the remains of a flying reptile quite near Mr. Marvell." Marvell looked again at the claw and shuddered. "There are warm-blooded creatures too—mammalian and others. And I have identified six different forms of upright anthropoidal creatures, two of them with the characteristics of humans. All have the same building blocks of complexes of chemicals."

"Yes?" said Liz, and Marvell could see that her eyes were alive with curiosity. The orange flecks glittered like fire in the green depths. She had looked like this when she had returned with the bit of flying film, he recalled. Waiting for Comp's estimate had almost destroyed her. How had he tolerated her? If only he had found out what she was really like—

The robot went on: "None of these remains is more than a year and a half in age. We have here, in this collection, bones which span a hundred and fifty million years of evolutionary history on Terra. And all of the animals were killed during the past eighteen months."

"Aye! I seed the crocodileys and the boggarts! I saw me old captain too—"

Liz interrupted him: "Sergeant, you saw only human beings—people like me and you and Marvell here—real people going into the Possibility Space? I mean, through Hell Gates, as you call it?"

"Aye, wench! And scaly monsters there in the Pit! And tigers like raging devils!"

Liz shrugged.

"Horace, it's clear that only one hypothesis can account for these circumstances!"

Marvell felt vaguely relieved. At least he would know what it was all about.

"One product of the extrapolation of a series of Probability Curves would give an accurate reading," agreed Horace.

"Speak English, not the Frogs' jargon or the Lowlanders' gibberish!" bawled Hawk. "I've a mind to—"

He stopped. Marvell, who was listening to the robot until Hawk's expostulation, saw that the madman's fierce blue eyes were staring at a point behind him. And the crazy Primitive-fixated persona was gibbering silently.

Liz continued with her infuriating appraisal. "We're agreed, then? There's obviously some form of genetic restructuring that's based on a knowledge of Terran evolutionary cycles."

"Quite, miss."

"D-d-d-do ye see?" Hawk got out.

"What?" asked Liz, eyes still shining with the joy of discovery. "What, Sergeant?"

She looked, and Horace turned too.

"The crocodileys!" Hawk yelled. "It's the crocodileys come for poor old Hawk!"

"Oh, no!" yelped Marvell.

Liz looked. *Crocodiles?* Was the Primitive right about this too? Then she saw them. Her analytical mind immediately condemned Hawk's report as inaccurate; whatever the reptiles were, there was perhaps fifty million years of evolution ahead of them before they could be called crocodiles. Larger than the Terrestrial reptile of that name, they were more fearsome, slower, more *basic* things. Their malevolent intent was unquestionable.

It took Liz only perhaps a second to note Hawk's error and make her own guess about the creatures' age; meanwhile, she was screaming and rushing to Marvell for protection; he was ahead of her, despite his cramp and fright, heading for the steep slope up which the dinosaur had scrambled. One look had triggered off the most immediate of human responses to danger. He had run for a height.

"Interesting," said Horace, as Hawk eased two grenadoes from his pack. "They must have sensed the presence of humans! Quite an extraordinary intelligence, to move in this way!"

The reptiles had crept up silently. They formed a semicircle around the base of the cliff. Within the semicircle was the dead body of the dinosaur and the little party of refugees from Talisker.

"A match!" Hawk bawled. "I need a slow match! The tinder's gone—I've no means of firing the fuses! Monkey—d'ye have the means of making fire? Quick, or Hawk's a dead Pioneer!"

"Run, Sergeant!" shrieked Liz from a dozen yards up the cliff. "Hurry!"

Black, unwinking eyes moved closer. The beasts were heavily armored, heavy-bodied, with short legs and webbed feet. Their snouts were short, though when their mouths opened in anticipation of food, they disclosed surprisingly long, clashing teeth. The sight of the teeth clashing was enough to make Hawk change his plans.

"Aye, aye!" he roared. "A withdrawal is the better part for now! Damn ye, Marvell, why did ye not stay to make a fight of it? And you, machine-ape, where's your valor? Ye had enough of courage when the captain and the giants had their contest!"

Then the reptiles came with a rush, concertedly. Hawk leaped upward and scrambled toward where Liz was recovering her breath. The robot effortlessly stepped upward with easy movements of its skeletal legs. There was a wild scrambling at the base of the slope, and Marvell stopped hauling his thick body upward.

Terrible sounds came to the panting humans. The beasts were fighting for their share of the great mass of the dinosaur.

"Aaaargh!" said the bloodthirsty Hawk. "If ye'd only stayed! If ye'd only helped me bombard the crocodileys!"

Liz looked down, horrified. It was all the worse when you realized just what the dinosaur had been. Great gobbets of its flesh were stripped. There was a snarling rush for the intestines. Over twenty powerful reptiles disputed with one another for the vast delicacies that were dragged from the dead beast.

What eerie intelligence had brought all this about?

"Come up, Liz!" Marvell was yelling to her. He was climbing once more. "Let's get out of it!"

His Steam Age impresario's clothes were in tatters. She could see one plump leg naked to the thigh. Half a patent leather shoe was gone. The cravat had been used to bind a wound on his wrist. The black moustaches straggled wetly down his face. Against the Alien's Possibility Space he looked less and less like a suitable companion for her; all of her earlier distaste for him returned.

"Liz!"

"Oh, go by yourself!"

"Be on your guard!" bawled Hawk up at the climbing figure. "Ye Frog coward, 'ware monsters!" He panted to Liz: "D'ye see him run? Why, he's a poor creature, your man!"

Liz retorted without thought: "My man! *Him!* He's no man of mine!" Then she recalled that she was speaking to a destroyed psyche, a Primitive. "That is, we're companions, no more."

"Aye?"

Liz felt the sergeant's gaze take in her appearance. Blushing, she wrapped a torn edge of silken fur around her bosom; she knew it was an utterly incongruous thing to do, when the monsters from Earth's past devoured an even more ancient beast, but she could not help herself. Much that was part of Liz Hassell's personality was being shredded away in this frightful place.

"Don't you think we should go up there?" she asked Hawk.

"Ye're safe from the crocodileys!"

"Horace, what do you think?"

Horace pointed to the top of the cliff, where Marvell was hoisting himself over the last ledge.

"I think Mr. Marvell might well follow the sergeant's advice," he said. "He seems to have run into more trouble."

"Marvell!" screamed Liz.

She was frozen with shock. The awful wrenching, smashing and snarling below were forgotten. For, as Marvell's hands were on the topmost rock, she could see a head slowly appearing over the rim of the cliff.

Marvell heaved.

He saw the black-striped yellow head.

Horace said to Liz: "Don't you have the feeling, Miss Hassell, that we are getting somewhere now?"

CHAPTER

★ 10 ★

Marvell was a grimly determined man by the time he placed his hands in position to gain the summit of the cliff. It was obvious that the robot held the key to the situation; it had tremendous resources in terms of pure energy, while its analyses of the unpleasant events that had caught up with him were of inestimable value. Horace, then. The robot had to be persuaded that Hawk could be abandoned. And perhaps Liz Hassell too. The robot would know the way out. Wasn't it even now pondering some theory to account for Talisker and its mysterious Alien?

Marvell knew that when the time came he would be able to reason with the infuriating automaton. The machines *had* to obey, eventually. Meanwhile, he told himself, he had to ensure his personal survival. Hawk could conduct his own battles, Liz could moon about with her head in the clouds. He, Marvell, owed only one allegiance. To Marvell.

Well, the monsters were now well out of range. Safety lay above. The hell with speculations about Aliens and their Possibility Space.

Marvell grunted, heaved, and looked up.

"Waaaah!" he screamed.

He almost allowed his fingers to slip off the rough sandstone. The great jaws were six inches from his nose. The stench of tiger was overpowering. A trickle of saliva ran from its mouth. Twin flashing green eyes stared with an expression of calculating amazement at him. Marvell made out the gold in the cat's mask, the glossy brown-black stripes. The eyes were yellow as well as green.

Man and enormous cat waited.

"Marvell!" someone screamed from below, but the warning was ten thousand aeons too late!

"Don't—" whispered Marvell, his native cunning once more urging him to attempt to reason even with a beast such as this. But his mouth was as dry as the red stone his fingers clutched, and his brain couldn't flash messages anymore. He was paralyzed with shock.

The sheer size of the beast!

Dinosaurs on the rampage, crocodiles from fifty million years ago forming a half-circle of clashing, greedy teeth: and now this slavering thing! All it had to do was reach out one taloned paw—

"No," said Marvell, finding his words. "No, I'm Marvell! I wanted Time-out," he pleaded. "It's all a mistake!"

The lamp-like green eyes were hooding. Amazingly, the green depths seemed to hold puzzlement. Marvell, never one to miss the signs of reason in any creature, tried again.

"There's a boy, there's a fine tiger! If you'll just let me go down to join the sergeant?"

He loosened his hold. The tiger moved, lightning fast.

"Aaaargh!" he screamed, for a massive paw had flicked out to cover his hand. He realized that the talons were sheathed.

It was playing a game with him! It reeked of the wild. The mouth was open now.

"Marvell!" He heard Liz Hassell calling again. "It all makes sense—come down!"

"Down!" squealed Marvell. He could smell his own fear. The green eyes held him in utter fascination. It must be delaying the kill for some sadistic reason of its own. What fearsome creatures haunted this hell-hole!

There was a scrambling sound near him. Marvell caught a glimpse of the scarlet fur of the robot.

Was it going to help?

"Horace!" Marvell whispered, mouth cracking, the skin rasping against his tongue. "It's a tiger!"

"Yes, sir!" the robot answered. "Miss Hassell and I are agreed!"

Marvell groaned silently. The bitch and the robot were

agreed! While he faced the terrifying mask of the tiger, they were holding a ratification assembly!

"Please!" he got out.

"Sir?"

Marvell conquered his rage.

"The tiger! It's got me!"

"Got you, sir? Really? I thought it was offering you a helping hand?"

Marvell fainted as the tiger's claws shot out. If it hadn't hooked him by what was left of his frock coat, he would have plummeted down the cliff by the same route as the dinosaur. Horace looked on approvingly as the girl clambered up toward the prostrate figure of Marvell.

Liz Hassell reached the top and saw what lay on the far side of the cliff. It was a dish-like plateau covered with vegetation, ranging from giant evergreen plants in a vast area of swampland to rolling downs and scrubby forest. At the rim of the plateau, there was a region of deciduous trees; she recognized, in one glance, the rich blossoms of magnolia and fig trees; there were large planes, maple and poplar. Such a confusion of vegetation! But there was enough of variety to accommodate the creatures they had encountered. There was swampland for the dinosaur, forest for the carnivores, even a winding river for the ferocious reptiles that had ripped up Hawk's boggart. Her excitement increased, for she and Horace were entirely in agreement about the nature of the Alien's experiments now.

If only Marvell could be released from his preoccupation with himself, he could use the sense of creative lunacy that had made him one of the most creative Directors of all to help resolve the Alien's dilemma!

"Is it?" she said, seeing the tiger exert its strength to place Marvell on the scrubby grass of the cliff-top.

Hawk, red-faced and determined, had his musket aligned on the enormous head of the tiger.

"Don't antagonize it, please, Sergeant!" Horace said. "It's a friendly beast! If you could put the musket down?"

Liz advanced toward the long striped cat. Its tail lashed from side to side. There was doubt in its green-yellow eyes.

"Have a care, wench!" Hawk said. "Put down me musket? Eh? Friendly? A beast like that?"

"Don't you see, Sergeant?" Liz said, forgetting that his persona could not absorb the nature of the situation. "It recognized Marvell. You did, didn't you?" she said to the beast. "You're down the evolutionary ladder too, aren't you?"

"I think caution," advised Horace. "Not too close, miss. After all, Spingarn didn't meet you, did he? He would know Mr. Marvell, and certainly the sergeant, but you, miss?"

"What?" snarled Hawk. He had lowered his musket. "What's this talk of me captain? What d'ye mean, monkey? Speak, ye befurred Frog!"

Liz smiled, for Hawk was afraid as well as puzzled. How would Horace explain the fantastic transmutation that had occurred? After all, Hawk had seen human beings enter the Pit, as he called it—recognizable people! He would not have seen what happened to them when the Alien began its tricks with the genetic structure of the Time-outers of Talisker! Of course, he'd seen the results of those tricks. And drawn his own conclusions. And how near to the truth of the matter he had been!

His Primitive mind had absorbed what data he had collected and made a pattern that fitted in with the eschatology of his own age! The Alien's Possibility Space had been, naturally enough, Hell. The monsters—unknown to the Gunpowder Age—were, of course, creatures from primeval fantasy. Boggarts. And what an expressive word it was! Hawk had assumed that his old companion, Spingarn, had gone to Hell.

As, in a sense, he had.

Liz almost chuckled as she thought of how she herself would explain to Marvell just what the Alien had done to Spingarn. Meanwhile, she would listen to Horace.

"Sergeant, there are matters that defy a reasonable explanation," Horace announced in a portentous tone. "It would need a Doctor of Philosophy and one learned in Divine Studies to give an account of the satanical practices which abound here."

"Aye, aye!" Hawk agreed. "A most desperate and fearful Pit this is!"

"And strange transmutations have occurred into which a wise man would not wish to inquire!"

As he said this, Horace pointed to the tiger, which seemed to be listening to the robot's voice.

"Oh, tell him!" said Liz.

"Speak on, monkey! I'll not fear anything to be found in this Pit! Didn't I bombard and destroy the boggart? And couldn't I have shot yon fawning tiger? Aye, Hawk's not done yet, even though he be in the regions of Satan!"

The tiger had completed its inspection of Marvell. It too seemed to be tired of listening. Liz stared in awe as its great lithe body seemed to swim toward her; the rippling muscles, the heavy bones, the beautiful and deadly markings had an hypnotic effect on her. Theories slipped away as she took in the rank smell of the male tiger. It passed close and stopped in front of Hawk.

The ears went back. The eyes stared straight into Hawk's morose, fearful face.

Marvell surfaced to see the black and gold cat as it fixed Hawk's face with its unblinking stare. He sat up. Perhaps it would be satisfied with one, even two victims. Hawk and Liz. There was, however, his own bulky form. He swallowed. Could he crawl away unnoticed? He looked around him and saw the nearer deciduous trees.

"Christ!" he breathed.

In the shadow of a gaudy magnolia was another tiger. And, almost hidden in the grass, two cubs.

Marvell knew why they waited. For the huge cat. It was keeping him for its mate and offspring.

"Sergeant, can't you see he recognizes you?" the callous bitch was saying. *Who recognized who?*

"Ye say?"

Marvell was delighted to hear the panic in Hawk's clipped voice.

"Oh, Sergeant, it's all an evolutionary mix-up!"

Marvell was stunned. Evolutionary mix-up? *Tiger?* He thought of a pit of bones and six species of identifiable anthropoids, two human. A reptile's claw. *Dinosaurs?* All in a Possibility Space?

Why?

"Oh, say hello to Spingarn!" the bitch said to Hawk.

"Spingarn! Not him!" Marvell yelled involuntarily. "He's bad news—"

"Spingarn? Me old captain?" Hawk said, deeply confused. "Where?"

"There!" said Liz.

She pointed to the tiger.

Marvell shrieked. A passing pterodactyl hissed back. He shrieked again.

"Me old Captain Devil Spingarn? What?"

"Be quiet!" Liz ordered Marvell. "Act like a man!"

"That's Spingarn?" Marvell yelled, knowing the bitch could never be wrong. "That?"

"I'm sure, sir," the robot put in. "A most extraordinary circumstance! If we take Mr. Spingarn as an element in the Probability Quotients and place him against the Possibility Space we have here, there is a most interesting divergence in the quantifiable coefficients—"

"Christ, keep it simple!" groaned Marvell.

"He means it's all a sort of evolutionary mess!" Liz said.

"Aye?" said Hawk, still face to face with the tiger.

"But it's a planned mess!"

She was right, of course. The Alien had done some conjuring with the evolutionary scales. It had made a space where humans gamboled—or ripped one another to pieces—as their earlier ancestors had done. The trick, the hard part anyway, was that the Alien had sent them down the evolutionary ladder.

"Hello, Spingarn," Marvell said tiredly.

The tiger turned. It snarled gently.

At the edge of the trees the cubs peeped shyly at the assorted group. Marvell suppressed a groan. *More Spingarns!* It seemed he and fat Ethel had progeny!

"Bring the family over," Marvell went on. "The kids'll be excited about Horace."

"Well!" said Liz, and Marvell could have sworn that he could detect a maternal interest. "Aren't they sweet?"

The great black and gold beast rumbled with pleasure. It growled commandingly, and the lighter stepping beast emerged from the trees. Two cubs followed.

"Ye're saying this, *this,* is me captain?" Hawk said, still incredulous.

"Transmuted by a satanical conjuration," Horace agreed.

"Bowels of God!" murmured Hawk. "And the captain's lady?"

"Yes," said Horace.

Hawk indicated the cubs. "His bairns?"

"Oh yes!" Liz said impatiently. "Of course!"

"Bowels of God!"

Marvell sat up.

Illumination came to him in a golden moment. He got to his feet.

"Liz!" he announced. "Listen! You, Horace, and you, Spingarn! I think I know where it's wrong!"

The tiger growled, a deep and interested rumbling.

"He might!" Liz said. Marvell had these moments. She knew herself to be a plodder. With Marvell, the sudden leaps of imaginative insight were often lunatic, sometimes so dazzlingly *right* that she was bewildered. "Horace, listen!"

"I always listen, miss," said Horace. "It's a part of my conditioning. I always listen to everything."

The cubs dashed to the tiger. It cuffed one of them playfully. The female tiger kept a certain distance between itself and the party, but she stared with great interest at Hawk. Marvell ignored the new arrival. He was busy with enormous, grandiloquent thoughts that he could barely begin to express.

"It isn't as mad as it seems!" he declared. "All this—there's a mixed set of vegetation, but it's mixed in almost a sequence! See, there's the swamp for the reptiles!" He pointed to the enormous stretch of swampland which glistened greenly in the middle of the plateau. "And next to it, there's a sort of Miocene setup! That's for the anthropoids, I expect! The Alien's put the two areas together because it isn't quite sure of their relative time-structure! It's got bloody great dinosaurs next to apes, and there's nearly two hundred million years of evolution between them! It's all mixed up! I know what it's trying to do!" He turned to the tiger which had gathered its family in a tight, comfortable group around it. "Spingarn, you know too, don't you?"

"Captain?" growled Hawk, hesitantly speaking to the cat.

He seemed to have accepted Horace's explanation of diabolical wizardry at work. The Primitive mind had these safety valves for disposing of unacceptable information: boggarts: a Pit: wizardry. Well, thought Liz, it was an interesting manipulation of one's incipient neuroses. If you couldn't take it, you said the hell with it.

The tiger's eyes blazed with interest. But how much did it follow? Was it Spingarn? And how much of Spingarn? Was there intelligence behind those great swimming eyes? Did Spingarn's overlaid psyche function underneath the carnivore's mind? Obvious, Spingarn-tiger knew Hawk and Horace and Marvell, but did it understand Marvell's inspired speech?

Liz listened as Marvell gathered his ideas together.

"Well, even if you don't follow, Spingarn, you've some idea of what I'm talking about?"

The tiger looked more puzzled. It rumbled softly in the depths of its deep, thick throat. Liz felt a thrill of terror once more. Suppose Spingarn *forgot?*

"Well, I know what the Alien's groping toward!" Marvell said. "I know why it's mucking about with the evolutionary structures! And I know what's wrong with its guesswork!"

Marvell laughed aloud in triumph.

"I *know!*"

Liz felt herself to be on a thin and nervous thread of near-exhaustion. She saw Marvell's fat chest, his splayed moustaches, his beaming dirty face, his thick bare leg, and one of a pair of spats which had survived the mishaps on Talisker: bloody, tired, hungry and totally out of place in his absurd costume, Marvell nevertheless had some quality that was lacking in every one of the bland men she had known. He was arrogant, not overbright, frequently wrong, stupid at times and invariably pompous: self-seeking, licentious and untrustworthy, he was *grand!* He had the vigor of a defeated emperor, the arrogance of a seeless medieval bishop, the cunning inspiration of a failed poet.

"Sir?" asked Horace humbly.

"Down there is where the Time-outers enter the Alien's Possibility Space!" declared Marvell. "Right?"

"Yes, sir," said the robot.

The tiger cubs looked over the cliff and were nipped back by their mother.

"Ye say?" grunted Hawk.

"And we know that the Alien got them to go in."

"Yes, sir," said Horace again.

Liz thought of the collie bitch, left alone in the curious combined agricultural and graser Frame; its human owners had simply upped and gone, called by the Alien's irresistible piping. And only Hawk had resisted! *How?*

"So when they got into the Possibility Space, it started shoving them up and down the evolutionary ladder, even if there was an evolutionary dead-end, like the dinosaurs."

"Ye mean the boggarts? Ye speak in a Froggish way!"

Liz understood what Frogs were then. A Primitive tribe. A vague memory came back of a race that were rather less uncouth than that to which Hawk claimed allegiance. She wondered again at Hawk's ability to remain unaffected by the alien's black-gold note in space-time. She was caught up, though, in Marvell's confident speech.

"Yes! The Alien brought them here, then tried to work out what we *were!* Humans, I mean! It's been playing some sort of evolutionary game—Liz is right! But it's not sure how to do it! Look at this place—it defies logic! I mean, dinosaurs hunting us! Dear Christ, and tigers! You see, the Alien's guessed something about the way life emerged on Terra and it's trying to weigh up its own cycle of existence against it!"

Liz saw that the tiger had understood.

It pushed a paw at Marvell's foot, but the fat man barely noticed. He seemed armored in his conceit and interpretative lunacy.

"That's it!" he cried. "The bloody Alien needs us as guinea pigs—or dinosaurs or tigers or apes—to work out what it's doing here! It's lost, but lost in a space-time it can't fathom!"

Liz exploded with understanding.

A lost entity, adrift in a chaotic universe!

A thing that could watch humans emerge but understand nothing of the processes that brought them into existence!

The Alien—whatever it was—had contacted Spingarn. That much they knew. It had somehow got through to that warped intellect, and Spingarn had obtained its assistance.

But to what end!

"Don't you see?" bawled Marvell, and he was all Plot Director now. Liz could see him groping for the lighted cigar. None came, and his hands scrabbled at the remains of his frock coat. "Liz! Horace! My old colleague, Spingarn! And Ethel! And you, Sergeant Hawk!"

He waited.

Liz knew that he loved such moments. Suspense. Just like the time he had unveiled the fliers with their steam engines and howitzers. It was impossible that they should lift off the ground. But Spingarn had got the machines to master the technology of steam to such an extent that the string and plywood-winged airplanes had lumbered and heaved themselves into the air, crew, guns, coal, water tanks and all!

"Yes, Marvell?" she cried.

"Why, the Alien's trying—"

He had stopped. Even the robot had lost its impassivity. Hawk glowered, against his will interested in Marvell's impassioned explanation.

Marvell seemed to have something stuck in his throat.

"—trying urgle-urgoo—"

Liz saw him clutch the base of his skull.

"Sir?" asked the robot. "The Alien, you were saying?"

"—uggow—" Marvell gasped.

Now he had both hands at the back of his neck.

"—ogg-uffoo—"

Liz groaned, defeated. She saw a strangely witless expression cloud Marvell's eyes. His forehead was awash with sweat. His arms sank down to his sides, and his shoulders rounded, so that he looked shorter, brutish, subhuman. Hair sprouted on his gleaming skull.

"—uffaw-oogg!" Marvell got out.

His eyes were cunning, his whole demeanor loutish.

"Sir?" the robot said.

Instinctively, Hawk was adjusting the priming of his musket. Liz could see religious awe in his fierce blue eyes. The tiger snorted, and the cubs raced to it. The female glared at Marvell.

"Not now," Liz said. "You were just telling us—"

Marvell's gaze turned to her.

A vicious pain blasted loose inside her head. Her hands went to a point just below the base of her skull. For perhaps a half-second she understood what was happening. Chemical engineering. A genetic time-bomb. The one tiny cell injected back at Center that would gobble up what was Liz Hassell's mind and replace it with another!

That single cell would multiply in a microsecond until it had eaten across the whole of her brain and set out on its journey, magnified a million million times, to the uttermost reaches of the nervous system! She knew it would happen, for she had gone through recycling before; but there was left to her a monumental spasm of regret! This was the Alien's Possibility Space!

She experienced a weird jumble of sensory impressions as her memories began to writhe away. Dominating them was a terrible fear.

She knew what had happened to the other humans who had been lured into the Possibility Space.

They had been thrown into blind alleys of evolutionary history!

Would she suffer their fate?

She asked Marvell.

"Aaag—offaw?" she said. "Uff?"

Marvell stared at her. His small, beady eyes glared from under the greasy mat of hair.

"Ogg!" he bawled suddenly.

Liz caught the stench of tiger and leaped as the male commanded. She saw a skeletal metal arm come out to restrain her and she dodged under it. A tiger cub leaped out at her, but she evaded that too and ran after the joggling buttocks of the male. His stench left a trail on the grass. She fled in the tracks he made. The trees were safety, though the cats could climb. It meant finding a stream and crossing so the stench was lost. Absently she picked at a flea in her fur and ate it. She did not lose a stride. She disliked the extra skin.

Marvell was at the trees.

He had turned to see if she was safe. When he saw that the tigers had not pursued them, he jumped up and down three times, letting out a wild roar of glee. Liz yelped too until Marvell knocked her sideways. She saw a caterpillar and put it to her mouth. It was bitter so she threw it away.

Marvell found a stick and beat the ground with it. Liz watched, impressed. She tugged at the uncomfortable skin that restricted her movements. It would not come away. She desisted. There was a stench of sweetness, so she looked at a tree with wide flat leaves. She plucked a leaf and munched it. Marvell knocked at a branch with his newly-discovered stick. It broke so he threw the rest of it at the long, thin red ape that was about to be eaten by the tigers. Marvell capered again, delighted with himself.

Liz found his diplay of strength and triumph overwhelming. She was afraid of the tiger, so she presented her anus to Marvell. He tapped it gently, reassuringly. She jumped up and down too. She tugged at the fur with all her strength and it came away. The wind blew on her skin and she snorted with delight once more.

Marvell turned to inspect her.

"Aff?" he said.

"Aff!" she grunted.

Marvell leaped up and down once more and nuzzled her deliciously.

"Miss Hassell!" A metallic voice came floating to them as they made for a thicket of bushes. "Mr. Marvell!"

"Ye traitorous Frog deserters!" bawled a threatening voice. "I'll discharge me piece at ye should I see your poxy arses again!"

Liz yelped and said nothing.

Marvell felt a tiny memory trickling through the layers of reconditioning. He tried to repeat the sounds: "Miss-miss?"

Liz bit him with an angry sharpness.

Marvell turned to the business in hand.

The mating was protracted and violent.

CHAPTER

★ 11 ★

"God's teeth, monkey, d'ye see the shameless whore!" Hawk said. "Lifting her skirts to a Queen's uniform! Why, she's worse than a Cheapside trollop!"

He pushed the more inquisitive of the two cubs away, but not roughly. The tigress bowled them both over and they hid under her belly. She watched the disappearance of the two white apes with a puzzled expression. They had taunted her, yet neither she nor her black and gold mate had felt any urge to chastise them.

The strange long red thing that was no ape and had no smell of life was making disagreeable sounds. Yet it was not hostile. Neither was the other, the one with the sickly stench of another kind of ape: this one was angry, it reeked of anger, but it had no malice toward her or her mate or her cubs. She watched and waited. Last night they had fed well. The remains of the carcass were buried not far away.

Meanwhile, there was the rest of the sunlight. She glanced at her mate and admired the sleek strength in his body. She gave a murmur of pleasure as the cubs nuzzled her. It was a form of ecstasy. She listened to the sounds, and memories filtered slowly into her cortex.

"Well?" said Hawk.

Horace answered immediately.

"There is yet more wizardry in this place, Sergeant," he said. "I think you will understand that the Devil and his works have dominion here?"

"Aye, aye, true! With a vengeance! And what's left to

poor old Hawk? With his captain magicked away into a beast of the forest and doxies shaking their poxy flanks at him! Tell me, ye Oxford and Cambridge ape-machine! Eh? Ye've the learning of the universities, have ye? How comes it that ye've let the Frogs escape? *And* insult a Queen's man?"

Hawk patted the tiger roughly. It nudged him.

"Why, Sergeant, the poor man Mr. Marvell and his young lady companion are the victims of wizardry, as I've told you. You must understand that their brains have been, ah, recycled, that is," he went on, seeing Hawk's long mournful look of incomprehension, "their brains have become addled! They've had a memory-cell implanted in their skulls—"

"Gibberish!" snorted Hawk. He sat down and drew a leather bottle from his knapsack. "Talk the Queen's English, monkey!"

Horace translated the ideas of the Third-Millennium as well as he could into terms understandable to a Sergeant of Pioneers of the Gunpowder Age. But Hawk could not visualize the kind of operation that had affected Liz and Marvell. He saw it as some kind of injury, in particular a bullet wound.

"They've been shot in the head, monkey!" he decided. "Why, if the bullet's not extracted, they'll surely die of the fever! A pound to a penny they'll have the flux in a week and be stiff in two! And the butchers will try to trepan them! Many's the time I've seen the horse-doctors cut the top off a man's head when he's stopped a French ball! But none live! None!" He glared into the bushes, but the couple had gone. "Treacherous dogs! They're no loss, monkey! Why, Horace, ye say we've found me old captain, and surely it's no raging beast that I see here! A very docile tiger it is!"

"Quite so, Sergeant," said Horace. "I'm sure Captain Spingarn recognizes you."

"Aye! And the lady that had the wings!" agreed Hawk. "Miss Ethel, ye'll remember an old comrade? Ye call to mind the first time we set eyes on this malodorous land? When we came under the spell of the Devil? When ye grew the wings and me old captain sprouted horns and a tail?"

The tigress advanced a step toward Hawk, her supple

body glowing in the sunlight. She saw the brilliant blue eyes and remembered. White ape of the frightful stench that had been one of the pack—*one of the pack?* She could fix the voice somewhere. She touched his boot. A stinking paw touched her head and she flinched. It was smooth and vile. But she bore the touch.

"I think Miss Ethel remembers," said Horace. "But I should advise caution. The, ah, wizardry is such that she may forget she knew you, Sergeant."

"Aye?"

Hawk drew his hand back. He finished the thin wine and put the leather bottle back into his knapsack. The cubs would have come closer, but the tigress flicked them back. Her mate subsided, lying next to the seated soldier. She stood, fairly relaxed but cautious.

Minutes passed, with Hawk content to let the sun go down. Horace said no more.

Eventually he got up. He looked at the robot.

"Now, monkey?" he demanded.

"Sir?"

"Ye seem to know what this place is! Ye've the learning, haven't ye?" He snorted. "And call me 'Sergeant'!"

"Yes, Sergeant."

"Then I'm ready!"

"Sergeant?"

"Ready to march, monkey!"

"Very good, Sergeant."

"Well, lead on!"

The robot turned to him blandly. "Where to, Sergeant?"

"Where to? Why—" Hawk stopped. He glared suspiciously at the robot. "Why d'ye ask?"

"Ask what, Sergeant?"

"Bowels of God, ye befurred ape, why d'ye ask where ye should lead me?"

"Because, Sergeant," the robot said patiently, "I'm under your orders."

"My orders?"

"Quite, Sergeant."

Hawk thought about it. Aloud, but to himself, he murmured: "Adrift in Hell? Me captain veritably a beast of the forest? 'Orris the monkey-machine reduced to the ranks? And gut-belly and the doxy deserted? God's blood, it's a sore pass for Hawk!"

Horace did not comment.

The tiger watched, fiery green-yellow eyes alert.

"Ye say?" Hawk demanded.

"I do, Sergeant. You see, my instructions are that I should place myself at the disposal of the members of either expedition to Talisker. That is, to these regions, Sergeant."

"The gut-belly?"

"Quite, Sergeant."

"And the trollop that showed her arse?"

"Exactly."

"But ye let them go!"

"Yes, Sergeant." Horace went on: "The fact is, that they can no longer be considered as humans, Sergeant. In effect, they're changed into little better than apes. The wizardry," he repeated. "And with Captain Spingarn still transmuted, you are the only human member of the two parties. Therefore, Sergeant, I am at your disposal."

"Aye!" said Hawk, in command of a situation he could appreciate. "Aye! I'm the only soldier capable of serving Her Majesty! Aye! Hawk is the officer to take charge!"

"Yes, Sergeant."

The tiger that might be Spingarn observed the long shadows. It sensed the approach of night. Soon it would be time to drag out the remains of the kill. Yet it could not obey the instincts of its kind. Curiously, the stinking ape was a member of its pack, even though it mouthed disgusting sounds and excreted a sweat of horrifying impurity. The tiger could not leave the ape. It got to its feet and automatically talons flexed in the heavy pads, ready to rip and gouge. It spat noisily.

"Very well, monkey!" announced Hawk. "I'll give ye certain instructions, 'Orris, and mind ye obey on the instant! No more of your insubordination, or I'll blow a hole through your clockwork guts!"

"Sergeant?"

"Ye claim learning?"

"Yes, Sergeant."

"Then find a way out of Hell!"

Horace paused, for the first time since landing on Talisker betraying a certain anxiety.

"Out of—"

"Ye heard!" snarled Hawk. He hefted his musket, and

the tigress remembered a sharp noise and pushed her cubs away; the stick was danger. "Escort me old captain and his lady wife and the bairns out of this fearful place!"

"Lead you all out of the Possibility Space?"

"And sharp about it!"

The tiger looked at the robot.

"What about Miss Hassell and—"

"Deserters and vagabonds! Leave them to rot with the boggarts!" Hawk said fiercely. "Me duty is plain—it's entirely owing to me captain, devilishly transmuted though he be! Lead on, ye befurred ape!"

A low rumble of agreement came from the giant beasts.

"Yes, Sergeant," said Horace. "I expect there is a way of reversing the energy-fields."

"More Double-Dutch gibberish!" Hawk snarled. "Enough of it—lead on!"

"Very good, Sergeant. This way."

Marvell and Liz Hassell were hungry. They followed the course of a small stream with cautious greed. Not a whisper of noise came as they put bare feet onto firm ground. Liz walked with shoulders hunched forward. The slope of shoulder protected the vulnerable areas of breast and belly. The nose was much nearer the ground than in a human's walk; she picked up vivid smells, and her brain was alive with the prospect of blood and marrow. Trailing two paces behind Marvell's naked bulk, she had implicit trust in his food-finding abilities. But she was alert for any opportunity he might miss.

Like two white hulking shadows they disappeared into the dark shadows of a clump of hawthorn as they caught the scent of another kind of ape. Vaguely heard, the smell was potent. It was a male. A young male. Not large, but enough to satisfy their requirements for a few days. Liz felt the pulpy fruit hanging in her belly in her excitement. She needed meat. Leaves and grubs could not satisfy her. Meat. Blood and marrow and brains and flesh. Steaming lights and rich dark liver. She slavered silently as Marvell made a tiny grunting noise.

She knew what to do. Both she and Marvell had adapted with instant reaction to the searing shock of cell-fusion. They were beasts, shifty, rather weak beasts, but they had an alertness and intelligence that would ensure their survival, unless a mischance occurred. They were more than a match for the quarry they hunted.

Liz left Marvell at the water crossing where they had picked up the scent. She made a large circle to the right of the stream. Her job was to panic the incautious male ape. It sensed the presence of the hunters, she was sure of that much. It would have moved away from them, away from the direction of their approach. And then it would have hidden.

Had it been accompanied by the rest of its tribe, Liz and her mate would have had to run for their lives; but this was a solitary and heedless red ape. Maybe it had been cast out by the leader of its tribe. It could be that it was hurt. Liz thrilled hopefully as she thought of the ape encumbered by a broken leg. She restrained her greedy excitement and sniffed.

The wind was right. It blew a musky and terrified smell toward her. She was a hunched white statue in the gloom of the woods when a whimper of fright came from the red ape. The time was now!

A shrill bellow came from her throat as she jumped out of hiding. She trod down dead wood, deliberately snapping dry branches with all of her weight to suggest a larger attacker. A number of birds danced out of the trees shrieking warnings.

Far away, in the swampland, a vast roaring came to her. It was no business of hers, though. She thought she had chosen the wrong line of approach for a moment as she rushed toward a dark thicket.

The small ape had a physical deformity. One leg was shorter than another. Liz howled in triumph and real rage. Hate engulfed the terrified animal. It ran straight into Marvell's path, its yellow eyes wide open and hopeless.

Marvell raised the solid branch with which he had armed himself and brought it down on the red ape's shoulder. Liz leaped to seize one leg. She twisted as Marvell struck again at the head. The leg twisted slackly, for the little ape's skull was cracked.

For a moment, Liz looked down with something like horror at the small face. There were round, ridiculous ears. The eyes were turned up, not yellow but bland and white. Child-like, the young male was stretched out in a pathetic arms-open position. Under the overlaid persona, centuries of civilized living rebelled. She released the leg with a shudder. Her appetite waned.

Marvell looked at her with suspicion. Then he forgot it and performed a brief victory dance. He pounded his shaggy chest, and Liz expressed admiration. She slipped back two million years once more and reached out a paw for the little head.

"Affaw!" yelled Marvell, knocking her to the ground.

Liz took a step back and waited until Marvell had begun ripping the body with the sharp end of his stick. She waited until he had located the easily-masticated liver. Satisfied at her show of humility, he gave her a portion. Then they cracked the skull and ate the brains.

The tiger drew back into its primeval state as the shadows merged with one another and the dark red sun was obscured by volcanic dust. It needed water. The cubs whimpered twice at the tigress. She snarled them into silence. Her mate led, so she followed. But she too thought of the delicious buffalo meat they had buried the previous night.

It had been a cow. They had caught it as it drifted almost silently through a water meadow. Huge red flowers trailed after it, for it had fed, wallowed and lazed in the sunshine. One crippling blow from the black and gold cat's heavy armored paw had stunned it. Then she leaped, a streak of pure savagery, for the massive arteries in the neck. The cubs had drunk the pumping blood.

The carcass would be pleasantly fresh. It would have the smells of rain and earth. The meat would be soft and luscious. She growled softly.

Her mate continued to walk alongside the stinking white ape with the strange skins and the threatening stick. She hated the white ape. If her mate turned away from it, she would lunge once and strike it down. But not for food. These apes were vile.

"How far?" Hawk demanded. "D'ye see, the sun's well down in the satanical regions and poor Hawk's done for! Eh, monkey?"

"I estimate that we are at the weakest point of field-banding," said Horace. "It is just over there."

He pointed to a small rock half a mile from the base of the cliff where the second party of investigators had emerged after their engulfment by the searing radiance of the Alien's force-fields. The tiger smelled danger, or it recalled a moment of danger.

"Aye?" said Hawk.

"According to my calculations, the Alien—the Grand Devil, that is—has set up his conjurations at that point, Sergeant."

"Ye say?"

The tigress remembered too. Her belly ached with hunger, and peculiar foggy sensations disturbed her brain. She thought of walking upright and wafting through the air. Her cubs wailed for water and food. She wished to kill the white ape with the iron voice.

"Sergeant, I believe I can effect a short-term reversal of the force-fields that hold the Possibility Space at this point."

"Aye? And the crocodileys? And the boggarts? Suppose they come? And me with only a little tub of powder and two prepared grenadoes and no means of making fire now me tinder's gone!"

The tiger watched Hawk and then transferred its gaze to the upright dead creature with the bright fur. Unclear associations formed, swam away and then formed again in its brain. It growled warningly to its mate when they were fifty yards from the small rock. The cubs squealed. The tigress thought of the swift rush that would snap the ape's neck. A hint of her anger got through to the male. It nuzzled her to reassure her that whatever danger existed would be met by him.

"Would ye have your trick of bringing fire from inside ye?" asked Hawk, still searching for a means of lighting his slow match. He remembered Horace's contribution to the fantastic fight against the ghastly creatures they had defeated in their first encounters with the Alien's presence on Talisker. "Why, surely ye've the means of lighting the match?"

"Hardly necessary, Sergeant," assured Horace. "It's extremely unlikely that any of the denizens of this place would come here after sundown. The alignment of the gravitational forces that are being used by the Alien are such that the prospect of more Time-outers coming through is almost negligible."

"Ye say, monkey? Bowels of God, ye speak a strange tongue!"

Horace grew sensors in his glowing red carapace. The antennas waved gently for a few seconds. His skeletal arms extended telescopically and more sensors crept out to scan the depths and powers of the energy-fields that held this weird Possibility Space together.

The tiger crouched on all fours watching. His mate was alarmed but she obeyed his unstated commands; the cubs were frightened, hungry and silent. If they thought of anything it was the ripe stink of the meat buried not far away.

"Sergeant, I must explain that the Devil has command of strange crafts," Horace translated. "He uses the very elements contained in the ground and sea and sky to manufacture a powerful lodestone."

"Aye!"

Horace retracted the sensors.

"Yes, Sergeant. And this lodestone has the quality of attracting men and women! It is by this means that the King of Hell is able to gather together the poor creatures you see in front of you."

"Monkey, it is a cunning device!"

Hawk was most impressed by the explanation. Nevertheless, he asserted his authority without hesitation.

"Ye said ye had means of circumventing the Devil and his works, didn't ye?"

"Indeed I did, Sergeant."

"Ye have strange ways!"

Horace assembled a tracery of writhing, almost living, wires on the dome of the little rock; the tiger shivered, another memory trickling through the lobes of its brain.

"I propose to describe a pentacle of power hereabouts," said Horace. "Inside the pentacle, I shall make counter-conjurations, such as will altogether confound the machinations of the Devil!"

Hawk blanched.

"Trafficking in wizardry, are ye?"

"According to the customs of the philosophers of Cambridge," agreed Horace. "And also," he added, as he put the finishing touches to the warping device, "just as the eminent scholar Isaac Newton suggested."

"Bowels of God!"

Fascinated, the large cats saw the thin and dead red thing pour sunlight from its talons. Fingers of rosy dawn stretched to the wire and the whole became a pale, glowing sun. The cubs closed their eyes against the glare, while the tigress howled mournfully. She curled against her black-gold mate for comfort, but he watched.

"Black wizardry!" breathed Hawk. "Ye'd be burned in England, assuredly!"

"Sergeant, if you'd be ready to step into the circle when it forms?"

"Me? Walk into a wizard's unchristian den? No! Not Hawk of the Pioneers! I'll shoot your clockwork guts full of holes! I'll bayonet and destroy you! I'll have your monkey-machine guts for me leggings! I'll bombard and utterly explode ye!"

Horace concentrated as the darkness increased. The patch of pale sunlight increased in size, lapping beyond the small rock. Shifting traceries of power shivered within the orbit of the energy-fields created by Horace; the whole rock itself shuddered slightly, under the stress of force and counter-force. One cub put back its head and yelped its fear.

The tiger snarled savagely at Hawk. It feared the dead red thing, feared its molten talons; it sensed powers unknown.

"No, Sergeant?" asked Horace.

Hawk raised the musket.

"No, damn ye!"

Horace shrugged elegantly. His thin, high shoulders expressed regret.

"Under the circumstances, Sergeant, I have no alternative but to—"

Hawk interrupted his words, the old soldier's instincts ever alert.

"Be damned to ye for a cozening rogue!" snarled Hawk, grabbing the cylindrical grenado from his belt. "Here's fire!"

He had the waxy taper of the fuse at the incandescent pool of fire in a moment, and the greasy cotton crisply spattered into life. The sparks flew into the grass beside the tiger and its terrified mate and cubs. It leaped high into the air. Horace sighed and daintily flicked a small glittering pellet between Hawk and the cats.

"I have to use my discretion at this point," he said apologetically. "A small local disturbance only. A little neural-interference field, Sergeant—a mere dose of laudanum, which you'll forgive me for administering?"

The pellet spread its load of time-suspending seeds. The cubs wilted and fell against one another. Poised for a leap to snap Hawk's neck, the tigress felt her legs turn to jelly. The tiger had already stretched out a vast paw to intercept the potent little container, but it was far too late, for the quiet power surged into all of its nervous system in an instant, and the cat dropped its head to the rough grass. Horace took the grenado in mid-flight with a negligent movement. He pinched away the fuse between metal claws.

The amber and yellow sparks drifted down. The little rock's dome split. Conflicting energy-fields warred for a few seconds, and then a weakness developed. Horace had a moment to drag one of the cubs closer to the terrible radiance around the boiling rock.

Tall, spindly, red fur glistening, long fingers extended to pour power into his creation, he was indeed an archetypal imp. Hieronymus Bosch could have used him as a model.

The emptiness reached for the little party. Shot through with energy-bands of haunting beauty, it claimed them. They passed through a tunnel of vivid golden blackness, bodies floating grotesquely and turning as bulk and weight sought for a gravitational base. Horace congratulated himself as they left the Alien's Possibility Space.

During the days after the hunting of the lame red ape, Marvell and Liz had little success. Though they had all the cunning and strength of a pair of subhumans of a kind that had originated in Africa at the start of the Pleistocene period, they had not, in reality, undergone the critical refining of their faculties that only years of successful survival in a true savage environment would have effected. They caught no other living animal. True, they discovered a bed of clams in a warm, salt swamp, but their feeding was interrupted by the sudden swooping-down of a flying reptile. They ran. Insects, grubs and fruit became their main source of food. And even then, their lack of previous experience brought dangers.

Marvell scooped a handful of purple worms from a rotten tree and gobbled them, only to retch and splutter violently as their poison worked in his guts. He was sick for a day and a night, Liz watching over him fearfully. He moaned so much that she stopped his mouth with earth at one stage, for fear of attracting any of the voracious beasts that roamed the swamps and jungles and grasslands. Twice she moved away from him when she thought him dead. The second time, she returned and raised her stone knife. But slow memories of more humane days tumbling about inside her brain checked the hungry impulse.

He looked up and croaked a command. She went for water. Slowly he stirred into life as the next day passed. He shed thirty pounds of bulk and his body took on a vigorous appearance. They roamed hungrily until Liz stumbled across a vast heap of bones with some flesh still attached to one crushed femur. It was enough meat to keep the pair of them full and content for another two days.

They mated frequently. A good deal of the time was taken up by sleep. They took to sniffing out trails used by other bipeds, some of which led to rocky outcrops. On one rainy morning, they chanced on a half-hidden cave. Within, there was the rancid stench of decaying flesh, and also something strange: burnt hair and bone.

Marvell pushed Liz behind him as he glimpsed a wall covered in striking representations of animals. It took him an hour to summon up his courage. At last, he put a filthy hand out to seize one of the small, unliving paintings. He caught only hard stone. Retreating, he sniffed his hand. Liz took it and sniffed too. There was only Marvell's intensely appealing stench. They backed away from the cave like children who have accidentally strayed into a haunted cathedral. After that, they gave such caves a wide berth.

Hunger, however, was their continual problem. Fruit supplied only a short-term satisfaction, while grubs and nuts were often inedible, even dangerous. Liz whined her annoyance when they saw a troop of small red apes in flight through distant trees. Both of them sensed that they had been lucky when they caught the crippled ape. Marvell placed a finger in her mouth to console her; she nipped gently, but she was still angry.

Meat. Her mind was dazzled with memories of blood and meat.

CHAPTER

★ 12 ★

Spingarn surfaced to find the world different. It was as though his olfactory organs had been cut out and his ears stopped up. When he opened his eyes, a wider and sharper range of vision was available to him. But the subtle and powerful senses of smell and hearing were almost extinct. He rolled over onto his belly and stretched puny limbs with a strange slowness. A small sound of dismay came from his mouth.

"What happened to the—" he began, and then he saw the skeletal red figure bending over a woman still in the grip of the sense-blinding molecular-dispersal field. He blinked, conscious of familiarity with the woman, with the robotic, red-furred figure, but still with the cobwebs of the field hanging inside his head; the loss of most smells and much of sound, combined with the vividness of full three-dimensional vision after the tiger's flatter, duller sight, troubled him too.

He knew something of what had happened. He could recall the apologetic murmur as Horace threw the little missile between his mate and Hawk. And then there was the mind-bending zany dance of the particles. There had been a gentle afterglow of violet radiance, which he could still feel on his retinas.

"Horace?" he said aloud. "Hawk?"

The robot turned.

"Ah, sir, you're recovering!"

Spingarn got to his feet. He was a short man of great width of shoulder, something over the age of thirty and in perfect health. But standing on two feet was both odd and at the same time right. He felt too high.

"Ethel!" he bawled suddenly, rushing to the unconscious woman. "And the twins!"

He located the two infants, cradled in an arm by their mother. He stared at them, vaguely disturbed. Although he could not recall seeing the boys before, they were his and Ethel's, no doubt of it. It puzzled him that he could not remember their looks.

"Absolutely unharmed, I assure you, sir! The lady will sleep for a few minutes, the children perhaps for half an hour. But the neural-interference has caused no damage, none. I have calibrated the electromagnetic disturbance and found it well within the tolerable range. Sergeant Hawk's condition too is good, though with such an overlaid psyche, it's impossible to give an entirely accurate reading of brain-patterns."

Spingarn rolled the boys tighter into their sleeping mother's side. It was early morning, and there was a slight chill in the air. He looked down and saw that he was quite naked. For the first time, he realized that he was Spingarn again.

"Talisker!" he exclaimed. "This is Talisker?"

"Oh, yes, sir! This is indeed Talisker!"

"Talisker!" repeated Spingarn.

He was hungry. And why should he salivate so? And why should he think of a small hole in the ground which he had further excavated? He knew. There was the rest of the carcass. Ripe by now. Covered with leaves, and ready for eating. He thrust the thought away.

What had happened?

"I took the liberty of putting myself at the disposal of the sergeant," Horace said. "He was, sir, the only available human. I expect Sergeant Hawk will be able to explain the full circumstances of Director Marvell's and Miss Hassell's transmutation, but it will be in his own terms. I had to make the subject matter comprehensible to him—"

"Marvell?"

"And Miss Hassell, sir. She was new to Direction. She joined Mr. Marvell's team a little after the first Talisker expedition."

"Marvell *here*?"

Spingarn remembered the large and lunatic Marvell who had taken such an interest in his own career. Always eager for a new twist to an established Frame, Marvell had questioned him about the way he had sent Time-outers to revive the desolate Frames of Talisker. But the fat man was a sophisticated modern—he had never been inside a Frame in his life, to Spingarn's knowledge. Not once had Marvell so much as moved from the complex of Plotting arenas at Frames Control Center. He wasn't a man for working in the field. Certainly not here, not on Talisker!

"Yes, sir."

Spingarn looked about, took in the expanse of desert, the sand, the gradually increasing light as Talisker's twin moons spun out of the sky and the sun came from below the horizon. There were more urgent matters than the presence of Marvell and his female assistant.

"How long was I in the Frame?" he asked Horace.

He was unsure of the past. That was the trouble with cell-fusion. It hit you in one blinding second, and then you were whatever persona was contained in the tiny seed-cell. Then, you were in the Plot. But now he was out of whatever re-creation of reality had held him. He was no longer that other man who seemed to have had a different set of sensory equipment from his own.

Spingarn could not help speculating on what era had claimed him. Stray memories would keep skittering through his alert and highly-organized mind. But such memories! Why, especially, *blood?* Why was that the dominant image? And why did he have to look at his own muscular arms and hands and regard them with such contempt? Why, too, the feeling that he should be nearer to the ground and stepping with massive grace, alert for sounds that no ear could perceive?

"Frame, sir?"

Spingarn recognized the half-playful question for what it was. The robot was pretending to misunderstand him. In its pedantic way, it was implying a superiority of knowledge and understanding. It had been the same ever since the first time he had seen its conceited head and its bizarre fur skin. Always attempting to display its mental powers.

Spingarn did not show his faint annoyance.

"I was in a Frame. I came out of it a few minutes ago. You must have brought me out. There'd be enemies, or you wouldn't have used the neural-interference capsule. I still feel the effects." He did, too. It was like coming out of the Gunpowder Age Frame, so long ago, when he had first learned of his weird escape from the consequences of his actions on Talisker. Then, it had taken him long minutes to adjust to the idea that he was no longer a Private of Pioneers in the army of the English Queen. His calmness had helped him on that occasion. He had tricked the Time-out Umpire, Horace of the red fur, into helping him. "So how long was I out?"

"You were, ah, out, sir, for about a year and a half."

Spingarn looked at the sleeping woman. The infants were very young. As he looked, he had a sudden vision of supple muscles under black-gold fur. Why should he think of a slinking, exquisite beast? The vision blurred and he saw Ethel's mature curves once more.

"What Frame?"

Spingarn felt other memories surging for an opportunity to express themselves on the canvas of his mind. There was much more to Talisker. Here was a small oasis. Other, stranger scenes must lie over the horizon, beyond the unseen barriers. And, somewhere beyond all human consciousness, there was the other thing. The blind and inchoate power of the Alien!

"It wasn't exactly a Frame, sir," said Horace, and Spingarn knew that he had walked in the shadowy lands.

"Well?"

"It was a Possibility Space, sir."

Spingarn felt memories thundering through his mind. There had been contests just as deadly, worse because they had taken place on the eerie planet of Talisker, where grotesque cell-fusion changes had occurred. He knew the robot was gloating over his disturbed state of mind.

"What Possibility Space?"

"Why, sir, the Possibility Space into which Sergeant Hawk projected Director Marvell and Miss Hassell!"

Spingarn sensed a weird mystery. But on Talisker that was commonplace.

"Go on," he said again calmly.

"Sergeant Hawk went too, sir. And myself."

"You came across me."

"Yes, sir."

"And how did you get into the Possibility Space?"

"Ah, Sergeant Hawk had observed that the remains of the Genekey had been developed—"

"Genekey! But it was destroyed—that was the understanding! No more random cell-fusing!"

"I'm afraid, sir, that your agreement was unenforceable—after all, sir, it was a most, ah, tenuous pact."

Spingarn nodded. Horace was right, of course. His mind boiled with questions. Marvell here? That meant he had been dispatched. And the Genekey reactivated? And himself inside a Frame that was a Possibility Space, for a year and a half? And now he had returned with no identifiable memories, but with Ethel and a pair of sons!

"So this is Possibility Space?"

"Yes, sir. The Alien's."

If Horace had hoped for a reaction of dismay on Spingarn's part, he was to be disappointed. The brilliant mind was unimpaired. Spingarn's imagination was already leaping ahead to plan for the future. So the utterly strange entity that had somehow been slipped into the Universe and taken up residence among the ruins of Talisker had used him, Spingarn, in some experiment of its own! What did Horace know?

"Why haven't I any clear memories?" he demanded.

He would ask Ethel, and Hawk, once they were fully awake. Surely they would be able to recall something of their patterns of experience in this Possibility Space.

"I think, sir," the robot said contentedly, "that you should ask yourself whether or not you retain any *human* memories."

Spingarn's mind suffered a shock of realization. It was a sudden and brief flaring-up of enlightenment. No memories—just impressions. Impressions of a flatter world, of blood and clawing violence. Of steely power and long feeding and his face awash with blood.

"Animal?"

"Yes, sir. When I encountered you recently, sir, you were a carnivore. A tiger, to be precise, sir."

"Ethel too," murmured Spingarn.

She had experienced strange transformations since her introduction to the planet of Talisker! The random cell-fusion effect had worked a wonderful change on that first occasion. He remembered the swelling ripe breasts, the elegant curves of her legs—and the tracery of membrane at her back. *Wings!* In her surprise, she had shot up to twenty feet above the ground, where she hovered, astonished, her wings beating gracefully against the light breeze. And now she had been turned into a tigress!

Spingarn regarded the sleeping children with a more proprietorial air. Twins! He looked forward to hearing Ethel's comment when she awoke. They must have mated in the weird Possibility Space.

"I was a carnivore!" Spingarn exclaimed. "It means there's more than recycling! The cassettes couldn't have done it—it just isn't possible psychologically to adapt the human mind to such a way of life!"

"Quite, sir," said the robot.

"We could do the physical changes—up to a certain point," Spingarn went on. "But the conditioning necessary for even a moderate chance of successful adaptation is beyond us! We can't make people into tigers!"

"And dinosaurs, sir," added Horace.

"Dinosaurs?"

"Mr. Marvell went subhuman, sir. We all saw the dinosaurs. Sergeant Hawk destroyed one."

"Destroyed—"

Spingarn looked down at his hands. Blurred memories of enormous padded paws came back. Talons. Talons and fangs.

"Yes, sir."

"So in the Possibility Space humans have been turned into dinosaurs? Tigers?"

"Oh, yes, sir! There was almost a complete range of reptilian and mammalian life. Mr. Marvell and Miss Hassell had the characteristics of anthropoidal apes, somewhat advanced from the most primitive known. There was a fair degree of intelligence, with some toolmaking ability." The robot chuckled. "As far as I could make out, sir, they were not dissatisfied with the transformation."

Spingarn was dazzled by the enormous prospects.

"A full range?"

"I detected certain of the very earliest reptiles, sir, though I suspect that they have a very low survival rate."

"So it's the Genekey—"

"Yes, sir."

"And humans—"

"Yes, sir."

"Spingarn?" said a clear voice. Ethel was awake.

He heard but relegated the inquiry into a corner of his mind.

"All the features of random recycling—"

"Yes, sir, but extended."

"Yes!" said Spingarn impatiently.

"Spingarn!" the call came, more urgently.

He waved a hand irritably.

"Yes, but it's the same principle!"

"Quite, sir."

"Extended so that all probabilities are given a maximum degree of variation—"

"Sir!"

"Gawd!" said Spingarn, relapsing into a dialect of the Gunpowder Age. "Gawd's boots!"

"Aye?" said a familiar voice. Hawk too had recovered consciousness. "Aye, Captain?"

Spingarn looked around, to see Ethel disengaging from the twins. Hawk looked at him as she rose to her feet.

"Spingarn!" she said. "What is it? Where have we been? The babies! My babies!"

"Naked as an infant!" Hawk said loudly. "Captain, your lady wife hasn't a stitch about her!"

Spingarn was shocked at the immense conception of which he had been a part.

"Gawd!" he said again. He recognized Hawk. "Sergeant, we've been in a strange place!"

"Aye, Satan's Kingdom!"

Ethel waited.

Spingarn at length got out: "It's quite fantastic!"

"It is outside my range of known facts," admitted Horace.

"Ethel, do you know what we've been—where we've been? How we went? Gawd!" He shuddered. "And what we did!"

"I heard you mention a Possibility Space," Ethel said calmly. "I want clothes, and food for the babies."

"Ethel, we've been down the evolutionary ladder of mankind! For the past year and a half, we've been inside a mixture of Terra's complete range of pasts! It's all been re-created—and the creatures too!"

Ethel looked at the children. She was unsurprised.

"Tigers? It fits. I wonder what they'd like to eat."

Spingarn's mouth opened wide in dismay.

"Like to eat?"

He was stupefied. At the edge of the strangest mystery of all, she could concern herself with such matters?

"A little minced steak," she decided.

"And clothes for the bairns!" agreed Hawk. He averted his eyes from Ethel's magnificent figure. "And a dress for yourself, ma'am?"

"If you please, Sergeant," she said.

Spingarn said helplessly: "Ethel, the Alien sent us down the evolutionary chain! All the Time-outers are in there."

"Not quite all, sir," said Horace.

Ethel gave Hawk directions. She kissed the sleeping infants and moved them into the shade as the sun came up in a surge of yellow flame.

"No?" said Spingarn.

There was a most disagreeable sensation in his belly.

"Carnivores require large amounts of fresh meat, sir," Horace pointed out. "There was a low survival rate among many species."

Blood!

No wonder he felt queasy! Spingarn thought of the thousands of Time-outers he had committed to the re-creations among Talisker's desolate Frames. And of what the fate of many of them must have been. He looked with dismay at Ethel.

"Ethel, those others! In the Possibility Space! We must have used them—as—as—"

Spingarn saw that Ethel was unconcerned. Her whole attention was on the babies. In her beautiful eyes there was a reflection of the ecstasy of motherhood. Spingarn felt his heart wrenched by the sight of the still-sleeping children; and he thought of their diet. Crawling insidiously into his mind came recollections of Ethel ripping the tender portions of still-quivering victims.

How could she be so callous? Spingarn regarded her without affection. Women were so much more basic than men.

"See, the sergeant's built a little house!" she declared. "And a garden! But it won't do, Spingarn. I'll need more room. And some decent clothes. Isn't there somewhere not too far away where we can settle until all this ghastly business is cleared up?"

Spingarn gasped.

Ethel wanted to set up a home.

On Talisker, the grotesque enigma of the Alien's Possibility Space still writhed in the insubstantial dimensions of the Genekey. Marvell and his assistant were in it. So were the survivors of a hellish, disgusting piece of monumental juggling with mankind's evolutionary patterns. Dinosaurs that were once men stalked lesser beasts that were their fellows. There were flying reptiles preying on transmuted Time-outers. Women like Ethel swung from trees. Men like himself scuttled through hot mud to escape scaled horrors from the dawn of life on Terra.

The Alien had done all this. The blind and terrible creative force that had once met him mind to mind had run amok. And ultimately he, Spingarn, was responsible.

Ethel thought only of homemaking.

"Horace," said Spingarn. "Find somewhere."

Ethel smiled charmingly. Horace left at once.

"Sergeant!" she called. "Did you say you had a dress for me?"

Hawk came back with his clay pipe clamped in his mouth. He carried a tattered piece of clothing.

"Begging your pardon, ma'am," he apologized, "it's all there is. I kept it against your return after ye'd gone down into the boggarts' lair with the captain."

Spingarn looked from the cheerful woman to the phlegmatic Sergeant of Pioneers. Hawk too had accepted the bizarre situation with a wonderful equanimity. The last he had seen of Spingarn and Ethel must have been the gradual encroachment of the Alien's weird Pit. Devotedly he must have pitched camp at the entrance to the Possibility Space, awaiting their return. How was it, though, that he could come to terms with the fantastic enigma of the hellish regions he had seen? And how could a Primitive psyche such as Hawk's account for dinosaurs, men transmuted into tigers, gaping holes in space-time?

Spingarn saw that Hawk kept his eyes averted as Ethel shrugged herself into the barely adequate garment.

"Sergeant," he said.

"Captain Spingarn?"

"Horace explained about the Possibility Space—the nether regions?"

"Aye, that he did, Captain! And an unlikely tale it was! Oxford and Cambridge philosophers! Why," said Hawk, winking, bottle-nosed face lit up with a smile, "that befurred machine-monkey knows no more than me! But we know, Captain, don't we?"

"We do?"

What strange rationalization had the sergeant come to? What could have accounted for his wonderful experiences?

"Aye, sir!"

Spingarn was pleased that Horace had not been able to trick the sergeant. However he had explained the Alien and the Possibility Space away—and it seemed as though the robot had described them as the Devil and his Kingdom—the grinning soldier had not been fully taken in.

"Sergeant?"

"Aye, sir! More Frog wiles! They'll be at the back of it—we know, sir! But we'll not tell Mrs. Spingarn?" Hawk winked violently. "The Frogs and Satan?"

"No, Sergeant. I think perhaps not."

There was no confusion in Hawk's mind, Spingarn saw. He was still fighting a war that had finished millennia ago. To his mind, the tribe of the French had made a pact with Satan in order to confound the army of Queen Anne.

"Knew ye'd return, sir! Knew ye'd be a match for the Frogs! Hawk kept a watch! Hawk wasn't tricked into going into Hell! And when he did go, didn't old Hawk utterly bombard the boggart? He did, sir!"

Spingarn wondered what the story that lay behind this claim could be. No doubt he would hear of it again. Hawk enjoyed the discussion of his martial exploits, like any old military man. For the Primitive, it had been a successful foray, for hadn't he been instrumental in rescuing his captain, the captain's lady and the infants? Coupled with this was some violent encounter with a monster. Hawk's grin was justified. He was a hero.

"I'm eternally grateful, Sergeant!" declared Spingarn. Decisions came easily to him. "But I require more of you, d'ye see, I'll need to feel that Ethel—Mrs. Spingarn—is in safe keeping."

"Sir!"

"You will remain with the lady, under her orders."

"Sir!" bellowed Hawk, vastly pleased with himself. "And you, sir? Ye'll join us?"

"Not at once, Sergeant. When Horace returns, I have certain duties for him. You will accompany Mrs. Spingarn to the place of safety he has found."

"Aye, sir, but yourself?"

Spingarn felt a thrill of pleasure. He had always known that the final confrontation with the Alien had to be on its own ground. The mysterious entity could not reach out to him. If he wished to eradicate the strange and terrible results of his own meddling among the Frames of Talisker, he would have to enter the bizarre Pit it had created.

Spingarn had to be, once again, the Probability Man!

He would have to enter what Hawk thought of as some kind of Frenchified Hell and discover a way of bending time and space until he could impose his desires on the Alien that had been cast out from its own Universe a hundred million years ago.

Once more, he must go into the Pit.

Ethel seemed not to have heard the conversation, and Spingarn had dismissed her entirely from his mind as an intelligent woman; but she had been listening.

"Spingarn!" she said, and to his astonishment he could detect a shrewish quality in her golden voice. "You're not thinking of going back there!"

She pointed to the path of the sun, and Spingarn could see the shifting, uncertain energy-bands that had once been the radials of the Genekey.

"The Genekey!" he whispered.

There it was, the center of the enigma. But there was chaos, where once there had been a certain bizarre kind of order. Such terrible chaos!

And he, Spingarn, must enter it once more!

"You wouldn't leave the children!" the woman snapped.

Hawk nodded approval.

Spingarn temporized, his mind suffused with the seas of uncertainty before him.

"Not at once, my dear," he said.

Recognizing a position of advantage, Ethel smiled.

"Then carry the twins," she told him. "Here's Horace."

Days passed, and Marvell grew thin. Liz lost some of her small measure of excess weight too. Their hair was thickly matted. They learned how to deal with lice and other minor annoyances. A pattern of life imposed itself on them. They slept when the sun was hot, and during the night they either shivered together, afraid and cold, or slunk away from the dangers of prowlers and creeping things. A ferocious electrical storm panicked many of the jungle-dwellers one night. Many of them made for the open grasslands, and, to Marvell's delight, a soft turtle-like mammal flopped down beside him exhaustedly. They gorged themselves until a pair of huge snakes discovered them and their prey. They had to run once more, furious and still unsatisfied.

They were very cunning by this time.

CHAPTER

★ 13 ★

Horace made some difficulty about using his more sophisticated circuitry to get them across the barriers between Hawk's oasis and the retreat he had found; but Spingarn firmly put him down. It was imperative to settle the children—still asleep in his strong arms—and Ethel before beginning the ultimate experiment.

Spingarn strode across hot sands, crisp wet turf, through the streets of a city chiseled entirely from a luminous green jade-like rock, past the splendors of Terra's lurid pasts as they had been re-created during the wild years of Talisker's first experiments: more and more he felt the pull of his destiny. He was almost suffocated by the thought of the glittering whorls of the ruined Genekey. All that had passed on Talisker echoed in his mind. The arrival of that first small expedition—himself, Ethel, Sergeant Hawk and the red-furred automaton. That first sight of the strange road in the sky that was no road but a traveling, rearing barrier! The ghastly thyroid giants, those that had battered a weird rhythm as they called for blood!

And what was Marvell's place in all this?

A terrible impatience possessed Spingarn. His thin face and iron muscles shuddered with the forces boiling in his brain. He was like a magnificent horse that senses the coming trial of speed and power. Yet none of his inner turmoil showed to the others. Spingarn was a man of dedication and iron resolve; he had learned, during the incredible years of the Frames, to control his emotions.

They came to a small fragment of peace after half a

day's march. It was a green and pleasant stretch of country, with a few small farmsteads of weathered gray stone. They were deserted. The only sign of life was in the thick hedgerows, from which beady eyes looked out with surprise. Horace indicated a substantial dwelling in good condition.

"I thought this would be the most suitable," he said. "I managed to locate three cows, one recently calved. They were afraid, so I took the liberty of inducing a slight state of hallucination. They have unpleasant memories of the graser-mines which littered this area, sir."

"Grasers?" Spingarn frowned.

Ethel inspected the farmhouse with Hawk.

"There was some kind of Frame-Shift at one time, sir. The grasers would have drifted through a barrier. I cleared them, sir."

"I remember this place," said Spingarn. It was a small re-creation of a bit of pastoral Terra. Some Time-outers had found and farmed it. But the ditches were blocked, and the vegeatable gardens overrun. But grasers! Well, thought Spingarn, dismissing the idea, Talisker was a planet of the unexpected. In his arms the twin infants showed signs of returning consciousness.

Ethel called from an upstairs window: "It's fine, Spingarn! Bring the boys in!"

Horace turned as a sound came from one of the outbuildings. Spingarn's reaction was slower, but it was still extremely fast.

It was an animal of some kind, he was sure.

The twins opened their eyes, first the older boy, who was heavier than the other. He had a squarish chin and Spingarn's solid frame. They mewled at the light, and Spingarn knew how the world had altered for them. He kept his eyes on the outbuilding. Then he saw the cringing white and black collie bitch that recognized the smell of human beings and wanted companionship.

"Spingarn!" Ethel called. "There's clothes here—and food! I'll feed them if they're waking up!" Spingarn heard Ethel giving Hawk precise instructions about water and firewood. Soon she would have a broom in her hands. Domesticity! Who would have thought that fat little Ethel, who had been one of his assistants in the days of Direction, would turn into such a splendidly proportioned matron!

"Coming!" he called.

The twins realized that they were in his arms. They glared fiercely from hostile eyes, puzzled and alarmed, yet drawn to the brown face. They struggled to be released. Spingarn laughed at them with great pleasure. He put them down, and they mewled sadly.

"Mr. Marvell and Miss Hassell passed through this Frame," Horace informed Spingarn. "The animal made contact with them, but it refused to use an adapted graser-beam to gain access to the contiguous Frame."

Spingarn listened with only half his attention, for the boys were trying to crawl. The smaller boy, who had his mother's astonishingly blue eyes, propped himself against the other and tried to get onto his feet. They looked at the ground, the sky, Spingarn, their own brown hands, the direction from which their mother had shouted, and back to one another. They stared in wonder at themselves, and then they saw the collie bitch.

It knew children. It advanced, tail waving furiously and mouth grinning in delight.

Horace began a report on the resources of the farm, but Spingarn waved him into silence. The robot was deeply offended, its whole posture one of distaste for the way Spingarn was disregarding his duties. He was absorbed in the behavior of the twins.

They were unsure of themselves, but they seemed to have retained the instincts of the tiger. After all, thought Spingarn, they knew only one way of life. He was alarmed for a moment when he thought of the subtle and violent effects of the Alien's transmutation of himself, Ethel and the Time-outers of Talisker; but he checked his anxieties. The boys were human, with human intelligence. Stronger than normal infants of only nine months or so, they had the memories of tigers and the appearance of mankind.

The beast in them won for the moment.

When the collie reached them, they moved each to one side. Spingarn felt waves of amusement as they bared two tiny teeth each. The collie sensed that something was wrong. She turned to the older boy. The other would have tried to leap onto her back had Spingarn not swept him up. His blue eyes flashed hate and Spingarn dissolved into laughter.

The other twin became a normal human infant. It sat back on its buttocks and poked a finger at the collie's long face. It licked him, delighted.

"Spingarn!" Ethel called impatiently. "They are awake! I want them—they're filthy!"

Hawk came out of the house, his satisfied grin gone. He was carrying two zinc buckets and a set of clothes.

"Your lady sent these out, sir," he reported. "Not the rightful uniform for ye, Captain, but needs must when orders come!" Hawk frowned at Horace. "Monkey, we'll have some duties for you! Here, fill the buckets! And see to the blocked spring in the yard!"

Spingarn nodded to the robot.

"We'll spend a day or two in putting the place to rights," he told the sergeant and Horace.

"Spingarn!" Ethel said again, this time with an edge of warning.

The twins knew the voice now. They shouted back and pulled at Spingarn's hair until he moved. The bitch followed, tongue hanging out. A low mournful noise sounded from the barn. The cows needed milking.

Spingarn shook his head. It was a strange transition. Beast to farmer in one day. He thought of the glittering seas of energy that indicated the Alien's presence on Talisker and swallowed down his excitement.

A few days, he promised himself. No more.

Marvell grunted to Liz one dismal morning when they were almost starving. He indicated the terrible swamplands. She came down from the hollow oak. There were no grubs, no eggs, no helpless chicks. Marvell posed a question. She opened her mouth to show that she had not eaten secretly. He grunted again.

She fell in behind him. They stepped lightly, both very afraid. Marvell had fashioned two clubs. Each was made of a stick and a stone. His was larger. But Liz could swing her primitive ax with some dexterity.

When they reached the edge of the swampland, they listened. Evil, slithering sounds came from the giant evergreens. Red eyes looked alertly around for lesser horrors that could provide food. Liz and Marvell were mud-covered themselves. The shadows of heavy-leaved bushes covered them. They were invisible.

"Uffaw," whispered Marvell.

Liz visualized large green eggs stuffed with delicious golden goo. They had found one some time before. Its reptilian parent had, apparently, forgotten its existence. They edged from the shadows, finding submerged foliage and dead logs with their bare feet.

A long, heavy-boned snake rippled near them. Its head turned to them, then it looked away. Marvell's stone club was firm in his hand. Liz contemplated flight. But Marvell's hand touched her anus and she was calm again.

They were looking for an unguarded dinosaur egg.

They were aglow with hunger and hope.

"Uff!" Marvell exclaimed.

Liz cowered.

Beneath the slime of the running mud, a vast submarine wave showed the passage of one of the cow-like monsters. It was feeding on succulent roots. Would it have a nest hereabouts?

Marvell slavered. Saliva ran down his ponderous jaw. Liz reacted by munching on her tangled, greasy hair.

There was a new sound, and a young fifty-foot high evergreen toppled. Marvell and Liz froze, horrified. The armored snout of a hunting dinosaur pushed through the smaller growth.

They ran back toward the forest, hunger forgotten. Liz dropped her club and knew Marvell would beat her. The ferocious roar of the carnivorous dinosaur surged around them. It was hunting the swimming, unaware, slow-moving monster.

Deeply disappointed, they stopped about a mile from the central swamp. Marvell held up his club and grunted. Liz cowered and stroked his belly. He hit her with his fist. It was a bad day.

Dazed, Liz felt a shadowy plan emerging. She had already dismissed the savage blow from her mind. With a lithe jerk she was on her feet. Marvell caught a grub and munched it. She snorted rapidly, outlining her plan. His small black eyes focused unintelligently on her dirty, weather-beaten face.

"Aff?" he said.

With considerable patience, Liz explained once more.

Marvell bit her affectionately when she had done.

She pushed him away. She was too hungry for mating.

She pointed to a trail.

They slipped along like hunting dogs.

After ten days of mounting impatience, Spingarn told Ethel that he was going. She did not raise any objection, but she insisted on being heard.

"I'm not going," she told him. "I know you didn't intend that I should, but I want to be sure you've thought it all out. You see, you still jump into things, Spingarn! I know we came out of the other thing reasonably well, but going too near the Genekey ruins was a crazy thing to do. I mean, we'd sent Horace off with the specifications, just as you planned, but we needn't have set out immediately to contact the Alien. We could have waited. It might have worked out some way of orienting itself, given time."

Spingarn listened, knowing she was wrong. When he had approached the Genekey ruins eighteen months before it was with the deliberate plan of contacting the Alien, and that, as soon as possible. The Alien had been the victim of some kind of disposal plot in a far distant time. For a hundred million years it had been buried. Once it had learned of the existence of other sentient beings, it was anxious to achieve a living existence itself. It was impatient to *be*.

The difficulty was that it did not know how to live.

Immured in a different framework of space-time from that it had known, the Alien had wanted to know where it was, how it could exist, where it had come from.

And he, Spingarn, was its link with the beings of the Universe into which it had been cast.

No, there had been no choice, a year and a half ago. The only evidence of the Alien's passage on Talisker was the ruined installation that could reverse the effects of random cell-fusion. It was in those bizarre whorls of energy-fields that he could find it again.

Whatever it had learned of the human condition had been learned from him, Spingarn. And whatever experiments it would attempt in an effort to learn about the Universe—and its place in this strange Universe—must include him.

He had decided, on his return to Talisker, that he must face the Alien at once.

So, he and Ethel had become absorbed into the weird Possibility Space: and, into it, had come the rest of Talisker's unfortunate inhabitants.

He must go back.

"Besides," Ethel went on, "it played about with the evolutionary chain and where has it got to? I mean, what good did we do it?"

It was evening. Hawk puffed on his pipe and stared into the red fire. Horace stood at the door, a negligent and elegant figure. He listened with interest. The twins were long in bed. They still slept together, curled toward one another for warmth and security. But they behaved now like ordinary human children. Spingarn watched the fire for a moment.

"What good?" he repeated.

About this at least she was right. They had been caught up in the subtle trickery of the Alien's power. It had watched the transmuted humans pass from one environment to another, from one kind of existence to another; they themselves had been thrust down the evolutionary ladder and then up another branch of it. And they had been lucky. But what positive results were there?

"I know what we were sent here to do," said Ethel, "but we just haven't been able to do it."

"There was the Genekey specification—it made us a present of that."

"That was only part of it!" Ethel said. "You know as well as I do that our job was to try to get the Alien back to where it came from!"

Spingarn's mind rang with the thought of the strange and potent being's long burial. The thousands of millennia seemed to swim in the space around him, making the farmhouse's whitewashed walls a view into another Universe. There was a feeling of cosmic forces at work that was deeply disturbing.

It had known him because he was the Probability Man. His own shattered psyche had echoed its wish to know the *how* and the *why* of its awakening. And, for a time, he had been able to contact it. Was Ethel right? Had they altogether failed in showing the Alien what life in the Universe was?

Were all the forced sacrifices of the Time-outers of Talisker in vain? Spingarn struggled against the answer. Surely, by examining the cycles of life in its bizarre Possibility Space, it knew more than before? Hadn't it been able to trace the evolution of all Terran species from the first beginnings in the warm seas of the planet?

Spingarn said slowly: "It should know something by now. About us. Enough to enable it to localize itself in space-time."

"I expect so," said Ethel levelly. "But we were sent to do more."

"Time-out!" whispered Spingarn. "We wanted it to be able to call Time-out!"

There was a pause. Ethel turned to Horace. "What's your estimation?"

"My estimate is that the Alien has learned a little of the Universe. I assigned every probability a function and extended a curve. There's a slight bunching of factors which indicates some hope of self-identification, but in an indeterminate future."

"Not good enough," said Spingarn.

"I don't want to stay here indefinitely!" Ethel said.

Spingarn looked about the pleasant, homely room. Some families could be content here. But not the Probability Man! Not Spingarn!

"If it stays on Talisker, we have to," pointed out Ethel. "You're its only contact."

"Then why didn't it get in touch when we were in the Possibility Space?"

Horace made a tentative move to suggest that he join the conversation.

"Horace?" asked Ethel.

"The probabilities are that it tried."

Spingarn felt unguessable forces crowding around him once more. The Alien trying to get through to him, when he was a brute beast? Failing? And, disappointed, still trying to fix a point of reference in a Universe totally beyond its experience?

Spingarn thought of the twins' first reaction to the sunlight when they awoke. They had gone to sleep as cubs and woken up as humans. Their baffled incomprehension was nothing to the Alien's bewilderment. It might have tried to get through the beast's brain. And failed?

"So what will it do?" said Spingarn aloud.

It was a blind and deaf giant in a room crowded with tiny, fragile, infinitely vulnerable creatures. Where would it tread as it struggled to escape the confines of its impediments?

What was it planning as it tried to observe the few thousand Time-outers in the weird jumble of pasts and long-extinct monsters?

"At least think before you go back," suggested Ethel. Spingarn was freshly shocked by her calmness. He knew her rather smug smile was caused by the thought of the two sleeping infants.

Spingarn turned to the robot.

"Well, Horace? The Guardians gave you your instructions. What can I do? And what can you tell me?"

The brilliant red fur rippled in the firelight.

"My powers are limited, sir. I have been programmed so that I have minimal powers of intervention in your affairs. What information I have is available, and I have a certain amount of discretion in avoiding certain unpleasantnesses, sir. When the sergeant commanded that I find a way out of the Pit, I could, for instance, assist you and Mrs. Spingarn, as well as your family, because to do so would not interfere with the probabilities of the situation. But as to suggesting a course of action, sir, that is impossible for me. I can make predictions if you set up hypothetical situations, but I cannot cause any alteration in the present situation. That is, sir, I can carry out your orders if I am convinced that there is a strong possibility that you could perform any actions involved for yourself."

Spingarn nodded. What it amounted to was that Horace couldn't contravene what was likely. But what *was* likely on Talisker? And what would the Alien *do?*

Already the Alien had begun a vast and monstrous experiment. What else would it do? As it struggled to try to identify itself, what chaos would it cause?

Spingarn sat for a long time thinking of the way he had boasted to Hawk and Ethel a year and a half earlier. He had been convinced that he, Spingarn, could create a small framework of logic and order and show it to the Alien. How arrogant he had been! And how ineffectual! How little he had done compared with his grandiose schemes!

"But I have to try!" he groaned. "We can't wait for it to think up more experiments on Talisker! Ethel, the twins—think what they might have to go through! When it's tired of watching cell-mutations up and down the evolutionary ladder, it might decide on something worse!"

"There are certain possibilities," agreed Horace.

"I've got to go!" Spingarn said.

"Yes, dear," agreed Ethel. "But you don't seem to be the right man to help the Alien, do you?"

Spingarn stared at the calm face. Ethel had once been completely subservient. Her only ambition had been to glorify Spingarn.

"Not the right man?"

"They sent someone else," Ethel pointed out.

"Who?"

Even as she said the name, Spingarn realized that he had forgotten the Guardians' powerful intellect. They had chosen the one they thought could help in the Frames of Talisker.

"Why, Marvell!"

"And Miss Hassell," added Horace.

Marvell?

Spingarn could remember his last sight of the buffoon Marvell. He had been dressed in the bejeweled codpiece of the priestly hierarchy of the First Galactic Empire, a vast and wildly enthusiastic man whose only thought was of the lunatic Plots he directed. Marvell—Marvell to reach out to the Alien! But the Guardians, inscrutable and omniscient, had chosen him!

And Marvell was loose inside the Possibility Space, transmuted into some other kind of life form, together with his assistant!

"Gawd!" said Spingarn.

"Aye!" murmured Hawk in his sleep.

Ethel announced that she was ready for bed. Her hair was brushed and parted. Her skin shone with health. Spingarn saw the prominent bosom and felt a glow of proprietorial pride. And then he thought of Marvell.

"Marvell!" he said aloud, shaking his head.

Ethel smiled. "He had some interesting ideas."

She would not elaborate and Spingarn spent half the night lying awake and thinking of Marvell, splendid lunatic Marvell. He found himself annoyed at the idea of

Marvell being sent to solve the weird enigma of Talisker. He, Spingarn, was the Probability Man!

Before he fell asleep, he laughed at his own conceit.

He would find Marvell.

And, undoubtedly, the Alien would find him, Spingarn. After all, for the Alien, Spingarn was a part of its strange environment. Spingarn was a *function* of the Frames of Talisker. He was inextricably a part of what it had created. As Spingarn he could reach it again.

He dreamed of the long entombment of the Alien, a long and deadly dream, full of a sense of slow doom and the immense tread of the centuries.

CHAPTER

★ 14 ★

Marvell was unconvinced at first.

The female was too sure of herself. He could not meet her eyes when she bared her teeth like this. She stared too hard, yelped with laughter too much. Marvell clambered out of the deep pit he had scooped with such labor.

Seeing his frown, smelling his anger, she offered a finger. He put it into his mouth. Large, flat, yellow teeth closed on it. She betrayed no anxiety. He nipped her without breaking the skin.

She indicated the rocks above the wet trail.

He looked at the dark hole which was inches deep in water. There was something missing. He scratched his head and discovered a louse. Liz took it from him.

She too looked at the hole.

Then her bloodshot orange-flecked green eyes widened. She did not tell Marvell of her other idea yet. Liz had learned that too much independence of thought brought pain.

When the sun was down. That was the time. First, they would sleep.

Spingarn made his preparations with the care advised by Ethel. He admired her shrewdness, though he found himself disturbed by the change in their relationship. She treated him as a slightly older version of the twins. On her recommendation, he watched the shifting seas of the ruined Genekey installation over a period of days.

There was a regular cyclic pattern of events. As Taliskers haunted globe glided around its single dull-red sun, the strength of the energy-fields within the chaotic and stormy arena of the Genekey varied; it seemed that the Alien had left some form of time-device that was linked with the orbits of the sun, the twin moons, and Talisker itself. Regularly Hell Gates opened.

At certain times of the day, the hole through which the Time-outers had passed reappeared. Hawk had watched in the same way for over a year and a half, waiting for the companions of his bizarre quest. Like Hawk, Spingarn caught occasional glimpses of the transmuted denizens of the Alien's Possibility Space. Once he was a fur-headed beast looking back at him. It was waiting, expectantly. Spingarn tried not to think of the times he had waited.

Naturally, he interrogated Hawk over and over. The man's mind was full of his own interpretation of the events he had seen—full of tales of boggarts and trolls, fantastic alliances of Frenchmen and wizards, strange and terrible appearances of Satan's legions and bursting grenadoes. Yet Hawk had the military eye. His observation had been acute; it was his Primitive persona that made him talk in miraculous terms.

When Hawk was asked to describe Marvell and his female assistant, his descriptions matched those that Horace was able to supply. "Beasts! Beasts, Captain! Unnatural apeish creatures they became, with hairy bellies and long arms and the eyes of devils, and tails! Tails, Captain! Veritable apes of the forest! And shameless, especially the doxy with the big bubbies, the whore! Aye, and running for the woods away from Hawk's musket! Leave them be, Captain! Begging your pardon, your honor, they're naught but whoreson treacherous French deserters! And beastly too!"

Hawk was able to remember Marvell's triumphant yell too, much as Horace had recorded it. And even in the sergeant's picturesque language, Spingarn could sense the triumph of the man he had known as Marvell. It all centered on the game, as Hawk remembered it. There was a game in progress. Hawk interpreted the notion of the Alien playing evolutionary games with the human race as some form of military exercise, the kind of parallel he might have been expected to draw. One phrase, though, came through Hawk's lengthy narrative.

Marvell had called the Time-outers—including Spingarn, Ethel and now Marvell himself—*guinea pigs*. Experimental animals. Unfortunately, as Horace pointed out, Marvell had not been able to complete his assessment of the Alien's intentions or state of mind. His words had turned into grunts and incomprehensible bellowing. And then the two apes, male and female, had run.

It did not seem so absurd now that the Guardians should have sent Marvell to Talisker. The gross man of the splendidly lunatic mind had been able to work out, in a lightning analysis, what the Alien was trying to do. It seemed more than possible that Marvell would have the necessary intuition to go further.

Spingarn waited day after day until he was sure he knew the working of the black entrance into Hawk's Hell. He plotted, with Horace's assistance, every combination of factors in the series of situations in an effort to work out the likeliest plan of action; but, as he did so, he knew that on Talisker forward planning was laughable. The only certainty on Talisker was that there would be quintessence of the bizarre.

When the time came—when he was convinced that no further observation was profitable—it would depend upon him, Spingarn the Probability Man.

There was only one more thing he could do. Confront the Alien. Find Marvell, then confront the Alien.

He, Spingarn, must once again try to reach out to that long-incarcerated heaving mass of intelligence.

Marvell jumped up and down with glee when Liz showed him how to cover the pit. She was not expecting praise, so she had taken the precaution of climbing a tree. She came down to have her belly rubbed.

The first night they caught a small marsupial creature. It spent hours trying to scramble up the wet sides. Marvell and Liz listened until its efforts ceased. In fear but salivating with hunger they looked. The grass was disturbed, the frail twigs supporting it broken.

Large, terrified eyes stared back at them.

Marvell sank his teeth into Liz's shoulder in his excitement. She hit him with all her strength.

Marvell reeled. Then he laughed with pleasure.

They raised their stone axes. Marvell struck first. Liz

CHAPTER

★ 15 ★

Spingarn heard the slithering just in time.

A few more seconds and they would have boiled over his body, rending and snapping with greedy jaws. He had known what to expect, but the reality was worse than he could have dreamed. A ring of the scaled, short-jawed things had formed around him. He saw, evaluated and leaped almost in the same instant. His perfect physical condition saved him. There was the merest handhold, and only friction for his bare feet, but he had the strength and agility to use them to scramble clear of the red-rimmed eyes and the fangs. *Some kind of reptile, a primitive crocodile!*

But there had been a coordination about their movement, a synchronization, that belied their primitive natures. Spingarn looked down and fancied that he could see the human bafflement beneath the hungry stares. These things had been men! For a moment, haunting memories of another kind of existence came back to him. He too had waited beside this cliff for the chances of Hell Gates and what passed through them!

He looked at himself and almost smiled. He was Spingarn. Horace was, after all, right. Would he be right as to the probable location of the apes that once were Marvell and his woman assistant?

Spingarn climbed lithely to the top of the cliff and saw the eerie admixture of territories in which he had spent a dim, blood-curdling year or more. From the swamplands came a distant shrieking as some Time-outer perished in the warm mud. The apes would not dare to go into the swamps. Not when they knew the dangers.

Spingarn checked his course. Distances seemed different. The Possibility Space smelled different too. Where once a thousand hints of stenches would have built into a pattern to tell him what animals lurked nearby, there was now only the overpowering scent of the flowering trees and bushes. He wondered if he had been right to enter the Alien's domain alone.

Spingarn shrugged off his doubts.

Time enough to call for Horace once he had discovered the missing Plot Director. Marvell must be brought back to a tenable structure of space-time.

The twins had discovered water and containers.

Horace was kept busy filling buckets as they poured water from the kitchen sink to the stone floor. Already they had learned how to make him obey. Ethel came to see them after they had thoroughly swamped the floor. She bawled at them until the younger one wept. The sturdier child looked her straight in the eyes and poured a last beaker of water onto the floor.

Ethel was stunned by his resemblance to Spingarn. As she scolded him, she felt a thrill of fear. She called to Horace: "Shouldn't you have gone with him?"

"With Mr. Spingarn? Assuredly not, Mrs. Spingarn! He knows roughly where to find Mr. Marvell and Miss Hassell, and he is quite competent to bring them back through the Possibility Space entrance. It would be against my programming schedule to give more assistance."

"But the Alien's tricky!"

"So is Mr. Spingarn."

Ethel was still dissatisfied.

"And where's Sergeant Hawk?" she demanded. "I haven't seen him since early morning."

Horace's elegant pose altered. He looked confounded, as far as a high-grade automaton could.

"I'm afraid I don't know, madam."

The twins noted the tones of concern. The older boy poked Horace's leg. He looked at his finger afterward, unsure what to make of the steel beneath the red fur.

"I think you'd better find the sergeant," said Ethel. "I hope he hasn't any crazy idea of following Spingarn."

"I hope not, madam."

There was a considerable pile of bones near the game trail. The male gnawed absently on an almost-clean shoulder blade. Liz's eyes narrowed. She grunted softly.

Marvell stopped trying to find meat on the dry bone. *Game.* He put the bone down and reached for the stone ax. Liz grimaced at him. He put a hand out to her. She bit gently at a finger.

They were both absolutely silent.

Sergeant Hawk stuck to his task. He had listened to the red clockwork monkey when his captain asked the way to the Possibility Space. Confused though he was by the terms Horace used, he was able to follow the robot's directions. And so Hawk doggedly stuck to the trails.

"Bowels of God!" he muttered as he passed the ruins of the green city. "A very strange and wonderful place! Heathen, though! Far Cathay would be just such a place! But Hawk knows the way—the Pioneers lead through to Hell itself! Be damned to all Froggish wiles for luring the captain back into the boggarts' hole! Enough! Let the likes of the fat deserter and his trull stay with Satan—I'll not have my captain in there again!"

He chuckled as he sat to take his refreshment.

"Aye, the old soldier's the one that has his wits about him! I'll destroy, bombard and entirely subdue the Frog demons! And the captain and his bairns will be the ones to thank me!"

Spingarn sensed the presence of others. He was on a narrow trail that he could dimly recognize. There had been much rain, and many of the familiar smells would have been washed away: not that he could have read them! As it was, he relied on his inadequate hearing and his acute visual powers. But a warning flashed itself into his brain. He was being watched.

"Marvell?" Spingarn said quietly.

He had the little container ready in his hand. When he found the missing Direction team, he would at once dislocate their minds. A neural-interference pellet would keep them quiet for a while. He need only lob it softly between them and they would fall as the subtle trickery of twenty-ninth century technology subdued them.

He looked around, to see fairly open forest. A few grotesque insects swam through the heavy air. Once Spingarn caught a glimpse of a heavy carnivore; its lips went back in a snarl, but it had fed and it turned away. He looked up. There was a tiny movement of black hair.

"Marvell?" he said again.

They were in the right place. Horace had worked out the approximate location of the best feeding ground for this kind of anthropoidal creature. It was here, away from the hideous dangers of the central swamp, and near rocks in which the apes could hide from bigger hunters. They would live on fruit, grubs and the occasional fish or small creature they caught; their diet would be supplemented by an occasional windfall, as when a larger beast hid its prey for later feasting. Their patience would be small, their intelligence low, their foresight limited. At best, their tools would be hunks of rock.

Spingarn was amused at the thought of Marvell with a rock in his hand. A cigar was more his style. He held out his hands to show that he had no weapon.

"Marvell! It's Spingarn!"

Some echo might awaken in the depths of Marvell-ape's subconscious, just as it had happened when he, Spingarn-tiger, had seen Marvell's face at the cliff-top.

He heard a tiny, greedy noise. It brought the short hairs on his neck crawling coldly. But what had he to fear from two apes? He was Spingarn, a man of iron! With his skilled hands, he could quickly render them unconscious; and, after all, there was the time-bending little pellet, with its seeds of unconsciousness!

He walked on, making no effort at silence or concealment.

"Now what did the clockwork ape say about these causeways?" Hawk growled to himself, as he reached the strange mass of the barrier. "Climb over only when they were firm at the base?"

He hefted the pack onto his back. Carefully he inspected the glittering black walls that were more than walls. He strapped his musket over the pack.

"Aye!" he declared, finding one of a number of handholds. "The red befurred ape spoke the truth! I'll soon be at the Gates of Hell! And then, steady the Pioneers!"

Spingarn understood as he pitched downward. *The mud hadn't even looked right!* He had trodden on it even though he had been aware of its odd consistency! And why? Because they'd panicked him! Because that glimpse of black hair had been intended! Because Marvell and the female with him weren't just anthropoidal apes, but transmuted human beings of great tenacity and a terrible shrewdness.

He should have known!

Spingarn cursed himself in the microseconds of descent into the blackness as the grass gave way and the twigs snapped. How simple it had been for them! Dig a pit on a game trail, cover it with rotten twigs, grass, and then a thin layer of mud—keep the mud soft and wet by sprinkling it at frequent intervals: but no wild creature would have mistaken such a surface for the real thing!

Only if it were distracted from looking at the path would it move on—only if it had some other care on its mind that overrode normal caution!

He, Spingarn, had been distracted!

Even as he fell, he tried to release the little pellet. It flew away from his hand, into the mud. No pattern of neural-interference radiated from it. It slid below the water and mud, inactive.

Spingarn felt shock, pain, wetness, a clinging gooey mud. Bright waves of shock flashed into his brain, but they came and went instantly. He hurt in many parts of his body. Consciousness remained throughout.

He checked, moving carefully. No bones broken. Bruising extensive, but no serious damage.

A yelping, gleeful, triumphant shriek rang out.

Another followed.

It was the victory chant of the apes.

Spingarn righted himself and reached for the top of the pit. It was like a huge grave. He scrabbled at a clay soil, wet and slimy. There was enough daylight for him to be able to make out marks on the side of the hole.

Deep, wet scorings were on all sides.

Spingarn stared in horror now.

Other animals had been trapped in this pit. They had used up their strength trying to escape. Marvell and his assistant would be waiting.

"Marvell!" yelled Spingarn. "Marvell, you fool!"

Hawk made his preparations in accordance with the drills of the Pioneers. He checked the short piece of fuse with great care. There were no cracks in the greased cotton.

"Aye!" muttered Hawk. "Old Hawk destroyed the boggart! He'll make sure that Hell Gates close for good! A pox on all satanical Frogs!"

There was almost half a barrel of gunpowder left.

Spingarn had explored every inch of the pit. There was no rock, no stone that he could use to dig steps and handholds in the oozing clay mud. He had tried to make a flimsy structure out of the remains of the rotten sticks that had disguised the pit's existence; but they were useless. They held no weight at all. He could not drive them into the sides of the pit, for they broke off.

It was ridiculous, but he feared Marvell.

Marvell!

Sergeant Hawk watched the bowl of his pipe. It glowed cherry-red. All was in order. The train was laid, the powder packed down, the barrel to hand.

He saw the long thin shadow of the robot, but he was not completely surprised.

" 'Orris!" he said, chuckling. "Aye, monkey, ye're come to watch the fireworks?"

"Sergeant?"

Hawk indicated the barrel.

"Be thankful there's an old soldier to take all precautions against a viperous enemy!"

The robot's circuits sprang into rapid calculation.

"Sergeant, you don't intend to—"

The enormity of the Sergeant's intentions precipitated severe confusion in the sophisticated automaton's workings.

Hawk bellowed with laughter. He had always known the befurred clockwork ape 'Orris as a fool.

Liz peered over the edge of the pit. There had been no sound from the trapped ape for an hour. She hoped it had been stunned and then drowned in the rainwater and mud. Her mate pushed her to one side.

Marvell looked down and grasped the big stone ax tighter. He was not afraid of the creatures they trapped, for they were helpless. Not this one, however.

Something about the smell of this one was wrong.

There was a sickly and disgusting odor from it.

Marvell snorted.

The creature heard and raised its head.

Liz leaped back, teeth chattering, tail waving stiffly. She presented herself to Marvell, who reached out a reassuring digit but still she wailed in fright. The thing frightened her.

It was bigger than it had seemed. It stank abominably. And it was alive and unharmed!

"Marvell!" called Spingarn, recognizing the features of the Plot Director even beneath the overlay of anthropoidal characteristics. "Marvell, it's me, Spingarn!"

Marvell gibbered back, enraged by fear.

He hated the stinking white ape but it was meat; he feared its roarings, yet they struck some chord of memory: he was appalled by the confusion he felt.

So he struck out at Liz, without meaning to harm her; she screamed in dismay and lobbed a chunk of dirt down at Spingarn with complete accuracy. The mud struck Spingarn in the face as he was about to try to reason with Marvell.

Seeing this discomfiture of the enemy, Marvell's tone changed to one of triumph. He bellowed loudly, the trees echoing his yells. Liz screamed with enraged delight. She lobbed another clod of mud.

Again Spingarn's eyes were filled with thick, clinging ooze. He cleared the mess away. It was so ludicrous! Trapped here by a pair of transmogrified Plot personnel!

Marvell leaned down to strike with his stone ax at Spingarn's head. It was the first incautious move he had made since the abortive venture into the swamplands.

Spingarn saw his opportunity and reached out a brawny arm. Marvell was unbalanced, overconfident, perhaps too impressed by the female's success in hitting the white ape with the mud missiles. He yelled in fear.

Spingarn pulled, and the hairy bulk of Marvell fell partly on him, partly in the ooze and water. Liz saw her mate disappear. At once she retreated to a tree. Shrieks and yells came from the pit. One identifiable bellow was for assistance.

She advanced, ax held before her in shaking hands.

Spingarn felt fear-driven hands clawing at his face. Yellow teeth tried to fasten on his neck. It was no time to try to appeal to Marvell's buried human instincts. He struck with great power and accuracy for the nerve-centers.

Marvell screamed with rage and terror, for suddenly both arms were hanging numbly and uselessly, and his belly was full of pain. His teeth worked on the empty air and he tried to lurch forward so that he could bite the vicious white ape's jugular.

The ape struck again, and Marvell slumped.

"Aggaw!" screamed Liz, looking down.

Spingarn wasted no time. In a lightning movement he located the heavy stone ax, picked it up and threw it at the female's head. She dodged back, but a glancing blow was enough to render her senseless. The lighter, better made ax she had carried slithered down onto her mate's belly.

Spingarn breathed heavily and felt a lightening of the spirit. His fearsome range of physical skills had not deserted him. He was Spingarn, the man who had survived in a thousand eerie epochs, Spingarn who surmounted all difficulties!

He addressed himself to the task of cutting footholds and handholds in the side of the pit. Marvell's unconscious body would be a useful first stepping-stone. The buffoon' had his uses, after all.

Horace came to the decision that he should intervene as Hawk lit the fuse. It had been a tricky situation. What Hawk proposed to do was well within the Probability Quotients, but one had to weigh this against the Primitive's lack of understanding of the consequences of his plan.

After all, Spingarn was *inside* the Possibility Space, so he could not be aware of what Hawk intended. And Hawk was equally ignorant of Spingarn's reentry into what he thought to be Satan's domain.

"Sergeant," said Horace, "ah, Captain Spingarn is in there."

Hawk's timing had been impeccable.

The uncanny gold-shot black space formed in its usual place beside the sergeant's stone fortifications. Great whorls of power coalesced, and the emptiness that somehow *lived* flowered into being.

"What?" bellowed Hawk.

"The captain went through Hell Gates early this morning, Sergeant."

Hawk's pipe dropped from his mouth.

Sparks flew to the fuse. In a moment, the gray core of the fuse had burst into volatile life, and sparks showered briskly from it.

"Get down!" bawled Hawk. " 'Ware blast!"

Horace obeyed. Hawk jumped behind a stone wall.

The barrel was engulfed by the fantastic, blazing radiance of the entrance to the Alien's Possibility Space just as it exploded.

A huge rush of hot wind passed over Hawk.

Worse followed.

Molten sand spumed into the air. A shower of crazily spinning fragments of pure incandescence leaped upward, black-gold globules of uncanny radiance that swamped the sunlight and turned the sky purple-black.

Writhing chunks of matter were hurled high up, and Hawk could see the chains of things that might be animals whirled high above him. Linked *things* danced in a frenzied, interwoven pattern of evolution. To Hawk's incredulous gaze, it was as if the boggarts were gradually becoming transmuted into more familiar beasts as they progressed. For a moment, even Hawk's ossified and Primitive mind could grasp the Alien's massive design.

He could glimpse into its grandiose scheme and see how the basic chromosomes of the human body had been built into strange fabrics; how varying shapes could be built into the cunning harmonies of the new gene-patterns.

"Bowels of God!" Hawk exclaimed. "Hawk's verily hoist with his own petard! Me poor Captain Devil Spingarn, where are ye now?"

Spingarn felt the surge of violence as the Alien reacted to the explosion. Great waves of appalling violence beat around him and the two apes.

The pit vanished, and so did all sense of belonging to a fixed order of space and time. A terrible radiance invested the space he had possessed.

Spingarn knew what had happened.

Once before he had been in this non-place, outside the familiar dimensions, away from all that was comprehensible.

Spingarn felt even thought sliding away.

Molecules and eerie submolecular structures danced zanily into his eyes and out through the back of his head. For a moment, he thought he heard the female ape saying, "You must be Spingarn!" and then the zooming undulations of the Alien's restructuring of space and time brought an end to all senses.

CHAPTER

★ 16 ★

Spingarn knew the terror to come.

Three blobs of quintessential blackness engulfed all thought and sight and sound in a raging hollow space. Spingarn was aware of the wide-eyed, shocked gibbering face of Marvell-ape, and the astonished orange-flecked eyes of a human female who was forming before him, shedding fur and tail and round comical ears: the ape and the woman reflected his own awareness of the horror of *otherness,* the huge and sweeping presence of something so alien and gigantically powerful that they felt a worm of pure terror biting into their souls.

Marvell-ape squealed, all animal, but with a human incredulity behind the large, rolling, red-rimmed eyes. The young woman put her hands to her head in a child's gesture of tormented fear.

He read her expression.

It was worse than the awful blow to the psyche that came with cell-fusion, for the alien force burned with a furious impatience in every corner of the body and brain in a single clamoring, raging instant. And it was the woman's first time.

What Marvell-ape suffered could only be guessed.

At least, for Spingarn, there was a contact. The piece of himself that met the furious torrent of energy had encountered the Alien before. And, now that the thing had emerged from its eerie, enigmatic retreat behind the black-gold corridors, he knew how to communicate with it.

"Spingarn!" he tried to yell, but it was a soundless call, simply a huge projection of what he thought himself to be. *"Me!"*

It knew him. Of course it knew him!

Hadn't he found it? Hadn't he rescued it from its macabre, hundred million-year entombment in the deep fault below Talisker's crust? A fault so old that vast layers of strata had sealed it from the gaze of the humans who had come centuries before Spingarn's time to build the first of the Frames and insert into the rocks below the surface the vast dimensional engines that controlled the barriers!

And hadn't he formed a strange alliance with the Alien? That early, arrogant Spingarn, the man who had reactivated the Frames of Talisker had indeed formed a most unholy alliance with the all-powerful, blind giant roused from its antique burial! It had been a terrible combination of intellects, two beings from different Universes, both shrewd, cunning, dominant, malicious and wildly irresponsible. Together, they had planned the mad Frames of Talisker.

Vile and terrible results had come from that union of intellects! And he, Spingarn the Probability Man, had been ordered to right the wrongs he had done to so many of the weirdly transformed Time-outers of Talisker!

There was a reckoning to come!

The woman urged words, ideas forward.

In the confined and yet endless space that the Alien had created for the meeting, the courageous companion of Marvell-ape had recovered from the mind-gouging shock of the terrible presence.

Spingarn felt a glow of pride in this display of human tenacity. He heard, perhaps imagined, the words she spoke.

"Alien?"

Whirlpools of fantastic streamers of light and power writhed into the space. A semantic nightmare began. The woman screamed and screamed again at the unutterable strangeness of what the Alien was projecting as she asked it to identify itself. The pit of blackness was invested with fire and furious whirlpools of doubt, pride, fear, shocking bewilderment and, always, that cloud of *otherness* that was the hallmark of Talisker's eerie inhabitant.

"Gawd!" whispered Spingarn, and immediately the Alien fastened on this new idea and sprang ten thousand images of all Spingarn knew as associations with the Deity into the black-gold straining emptiness. Vast globules of holiness solemnly dissolved into one another as weird and forgotten memories of gods strode through the Alien's projected space. Gods bellowed, bowed, grinned, blessed, cursed, blasted the ghosts of their followers and chewed on their souls. Spingarn tried to divert the Alien's attention from his inadvertent exclamation.

"I am the Probability Man!"

The Alien allowed the racing clouds of deities to writhe away and the pit of emptiness was full of a vast unseen but vivid acknowledgment of his presence.

Marvell-ape was somewhere within the raging blackness too, a long-armed rolling-eyed Marvell that was totally lost in the pit. And the woman. She was there. Spingarn saw that some incredible chance of chromosome-structuring had brought her back into the human epoch, shuddering back down the chain of evolutionary history. Marvell was still stranded, but she had returned to human form!

And she was alive with questions!

Her mind almost completely disoriented, there was still the vital human force of desire for knowledge within the space she occupied!

She asked his questions for him.

"Spingarn, what is it doing?"

Confusion!

Again, blistering, chaotic arenas of semantic nightmares, as the Alien strove to reach to the two human minds.

Spingarn saw every moment of his doings on Talisker as the Alien dissected everything that had happened to him over the past few years. He saw himself aglow with pride as the first batch of Time-outers encountered the unholy device built as a Clockwork Zodiac. He watched arrogant, selfish Spingarns feeding data into the cell-fusion machines so that the terrible gene-mutations would take place. He saw himself the subject of one of those mutations, a figure horned and with a wickedly barbed tail that lashed at the thyroid giants as they reached for him with huge, blood-stained hands!

Spingarn formed the question once more.

"Why the Possibility Space? Why the evolutionary experiments?"

Pride!

The Alien was very conscious of its achievement.

Contempt.

Spingarn knew that it had survived the entire history of life on Terra. It was older than the oldest of Terrestrial life forms. The Alien was grotesquely amused at the thought of the evolution of his race.

"You needed me!" Spingarn bawled, unafraid. "You needed me! I rescued you when you were buried—you and I needed one another!"

Confusion again.

The *otherness* in the space boiled around Spingarn, and again he felt the fiery touch of the Alien's power. It bit into his brain like a serpent. The female screamed.

"Why?" yelled Spingarn, writhing.

There was a pause, and the thing's shocked refusal to answer gave Spingarn and Liz Hassell a moment to look at one another. Liz put a hand to Marvell-ape's shoulder; it accepted the comforting touch. Spingarn saw recognition in the ape's eyes. It knew the dangers.

"It's frightened!" said Liz. "Spingarn—I know it's frightened!"

"Of course it's frightened!" snarled Spingarn. "It doesn't know about us or itself or Talisker or any part of the Galaxy—it doesn't have anything in the Universe to relate to but its crazy experiments here!"

Marvell-ape gibbered softly, eyes wide and brown.

Liz pointed at Marvell.

"He's supposed to know how to help it!"

All speech stopped as the Alien returned.

The Alien's potent and chaotic presence filled the space again, and speech was impossible. It showed them how the ghastly experiment had been conducted, a weird seminar on cell-fusion and psyche recycling that stretched through three hundred million years of life. Spingarn and Liz watched in dazzled amazement as men and women reeled away, changing their physical characteristics in some subtle way that reflected their own basic psyches. Small, quiet women became vast sinuous reptiles living like cows at the bottom of swamps. Angry and sullen men strode down the evolutionary ladder to end as glittering armored insects, while large and quietly-vicious men became primordial carnivores. Spingarn and Liz looked to one another for reassurance, while Marvell-ape hid its eyes.

The Alien waited for a reaction.

"Why?" gasped Spingarn.

Pride again. It was a considerable achievement. An exercise of powers. The Alien had built something. It radiated a feeling of success.

It waited once more.

Spingarn was helpless. There was nothing he could do or say to the Alien. His simple plan had been to show the Alien how a small fragment of order might be made in the chaotic Frames of Talisker: it had responded by showing that it understood the complete and total sphere of Terrestrial activity.

"Marvell!" Spingarn heard Liz call. "Marvell, you know something!"

"Aggaw!" groaned Marvell.

The Alien indicated its mounting impatience. A hint of its vast bewilderment was enough to drive all thought of rebellion and helplessness from Spingarn's mind.

"Marvell knows!" he yelled to the Alien.

Marvell?

Spingarn saw a fantastic projection of Marvell, whole glittering sequences of Marvells winding around the uncanny emptiness the three ill-assorted creatures inhabited. Marvell, bald, top hat pushed back, bawling uncouth comments to his assistants: Marvell in the green-gold robes of a Mithraic priest: Marvell swanning through an asteroid belt with the graceful wings of the Solar Cultists on his shoulders. Arrogant, conceited, dominant, frequently a failure. Loud, violent, lecherous.

"Yes!" Liz Hassell's voice rang back.

How?

It was interested. It had reached the two human minds, and accepted that they promised help.

"He's a bloody ape!" snarled Spingarn, exasperated suddenly. "How can a silly ape like Marvell do anything?"

Marvell-ape nodded wisely. It covered its eyes and whimpered afresh.

"Yes!" Liz yelled. "He can! He can talk—we had

speech! It wasn't much, but we could talk to one another—we had a language! I can translate still—it's still here!"

The Alien waited. Spingarn could feel its slow surge of impatience. It matched what he had once felt. There was a recognizable anxiety in its confusion.

"Try," he told Liz.

Liz Hassell was herself almost tongue-tied. Here, in this impossible hole in the fabric of space and time, she was about to try to translate the ideas of a twenty-ninth century Marvell for a being that had lain deep below Talisker's haunted Frames! And the language she would use was that of an anthropoidal ape!

Trained as she was in linguistics, it was not an easy task. The words she and Marvell had used during the days of blood, mating (she remembered the mating with a shock of shame), and running from other animals still clung to her memory. The trouble was that there were so few words! A total lexicon of twenty-three words, some of them admittedly usable in combination with others, but none of them relating to advanced abstract ideas. So few words to ask how Marvell-ape could begin to orientate the bizarre Alien!

She held Marvell's hand and looked into his wide brown eyes. Spingarn watched. The pulsing sense of *otherness* invested the tiny enclosed pit of emptiness.

"Aggaw-aff?" she said.

Marvell-ape heard the words of the white ape and the sounds of his mate. Liz offered him a finger. Marvell hesitated. Liz thought he might bite it off.

She hid her disgust as he nipped her gently.

She was his mate, but she stank. She had voiced the sound of conciliation.

"Aff," he said. His male pride began to return. So far, since the world had vanished, he had shown only surrender signs. Now, he stood.

"Uff?" the stinking mate asked.

"Agg-agg-agg!" Marvell-ape said scornfully.

"Well?" demanded Spingarn.

Liz gestured impatiently, Marvell-ape watching with care. He did not like the abominable white male ape, but it frightened him. It could wound with its hands. He would kill it, given a chance.

"Wait!" Liz said. "I'm just getting him in the right

associative field. I'm starting with his notions of the good life—I'll get him on to food-gathering and—and other things. There's a couple of word-sounds that mean things like *soon* and *time-past*. I'll lead in to those later."

The grotesque conversation proceeded. Spingarn felt his admiration for the girl growing. She was an ill-kempt creature, not overly attractive physically, but she had a vitality he could appreciate. The male ape was watching him, Spingarn noticed.

It was strange to think of Marvell-ape jealous of Spingarn in this emptiness.

Time passed, and the girl probed with question after question in the gutturals of the subhuman speech; Marvell answered with growing pride. Did he sense that he was once more the center of the stage? Was there a hint of the boisterous loudmouthed buffoon in the pouting lips of the ape? A memory of Marvell's vast conceit in its wide gestures of hairy paw and in the straddle-legged belly-protruding stance?

"Anything?" Spingarn asked.

The Alien sensed a forward movement. It brought a baying, howling, billowing series of cosmic demands into the blackness. Spingarn reeled at the force.

The ape tottered back, dismayed.

Patiently Liz restored its confidence.

Again Marvell-ape strutted. More gutturals followed.

Finally, the anthropoidal creature glared at Spingarn.

"Agg-affaw-agg-guff-agg?" it demanded.

Liz soothed it.

"What is it saying?" Spingarn exclaimed.

"It wants to know if you're the one who's asking the questions."

"Why?"

Liz smiled.

"It wants you out of the way. I think Mr. Marvell's jealous."

"Tell him yes!"

Liz jabbered at Marvell-ape, and then the hairy squat creature got to its fullest height and intoned, in a triumphant call:

"Agg-uff-agg-fagg-uffaw-agg!"

"What?" bawled Spingarn, who had scarcely believed in Liz's abilities as a linguist at the start, but who now hung onto every clicking, guttural noise. "What does Marvell say?"

Liz had a beatific expression on her face.

"I knew it! It *was* all wrong! The Alien doesn't really know much about us—it's all so tenuous! I mean, it got its chain of evolution wrong—it shoved some of us down dead-ends, and it got the geological periods mixed up! I knew it was all so experimental! And now Marvell's told us!"

What. . . !

A whirlwind announced the end of the Alien's patience. A monumental, hundred-million-year-old period of waiting was in the cry of bewilderment.

"Tell me!" screamed Spingarn, his mind shocked into fragments by the shattering call of the Alien.

Liz reeled against him.

"Marvell says it's got to—"

She spun, her mind a battered, tormented thing.

"What, Miss Hassell?"

Liz Hassell mouthed the words, and Spingarn caught them.

"Tell it to do what Marvell does—"

"Yes?"

"*—approximate!*"

Spingarn felt a giant thrust of hope.

It was not enough, not yet.

"How?"

The Alien took up the query.

How?

Liz gasped: "If you don't have all the facts—*guess!*"

Spingarn exulted. It was Marvell, after all, who had seen into the problem. The splendid lunatic baboon-Marvell had solved the riddle of releasing the Alien from the desolate Frames of Talisker.

"*Approximate!*"

He yelled into the emptiness and felt the cold uncanny intelligence of the Alien all about him. It grabbed every fiber of his nervous system, coiling in and around every tendril of knowledge.

"You did it with us!" Spingarn bawled. "Do it with your own knowledge of yourself!"

Yes?

"Yes! Make an approximation of your own evolutionary

progress—there must have been one, whatever Universe you belong to! Transform your own genes or whatever you're made up of!"

It's possible!

There was hope in the Alien's answer. It was awash with something of Spingarn's own exultation.

"You made a Possibility Space for us—try to make one for yourself!"

Yes?

"Yes. . . !"

If it fails?

Spingarn grinned.

"Call for the Probability Man!"

Emptiness hung, coalescing into a writhing, living mass of pure *otherness.* Marvell-ape yelled again. Liz Hassell put her arms around it. Blobs of blackness congealed.

"It's going!" Liz squealed. "Spingarn, get Marvell put right!"

Spingarn understood. The Time-outers of Talisker must be returned to what they had been. Marvell, glorious ape-thing, too.

"Return us! Release the guinea pigs!"

The grotesque, quivering blobs of emptiness were steady for a moment. Spingarn and Liz Hassell felt a rush of decision from the Alien.

Agreed!

Spingarn breathed a sigh of relief. His mission was accomplished. The Alien had set up the weird experiments on Talisker to try to find how other intelligent beings adapted themselves against a fragmented situation. It had tried to assess its own being against their efforts. When it failed to make progress, it had extended the experimental procedures to take in the entire evolutionary history of the beings it found on Talisker.

And Marvell had sprung on it the dazzling idea of making an approximation of its environment.

Perhaps the Alien could learn enough about itself to allow a return to its own long-lost Universe!

Marvell-ape gibbered with fear and annoyance. The fear was caused by the overwhelming majesty of the scene the three cowering beings witnessed. They saw the departure of the Alien.

Marvell's annoyance came from Spingarn's continued

presence. Marvell-ape felt blood-hate whirling in its brain. Fear too, fear of the collapse of this blackness. But hate!

There was nothing any of the three could think or feel at the slow, terrible, sinuous unwinding of the great coils of power that held the Alien's Possibility Space in place. They saw Talisker lurch in its orbit, the sun glow with a surge of fire, the twin moons race around the planet in a frenzy. Continents plunged into the central core, volcanoes fifty miles across spumed in anguish as power-sources were realigned. Ancient Frames which had withstood the shocks of Frame-Shift for centuries crumbled into shards of luminescent metals. And creatures writhed down their own gene-structures and gradually became men and women and their children.

There was an appraisal of Spingarn by the Alien in the seconds that remained.

No farewell, no acknowledgment. Just a fixed, long Alien assessment. Spingarn shuddered as Alien eyes peered into the recesses of his soul.

With a rushing, colossal shock, the Alien plunged out of Talisker's space-time, away from the lonely, haunted planet, out somewhere into the Void to find its own destiny.

Gone!

Spingarn yelled with shock and triumph.

The blackness raged for a few microseconds, and then was gone.

Liz Hassell blinked in the sunlight. Glittering sand reflected the harsh light of Talisker's sun. It was daytime. They were near the oasis.

"Bowels of God! It's the Frog doxy!"

"Mr. Spingarn!" called Horace.

"Look out!" yelled Liz Hassell.

A lean and malevolent Marvell had launched himself at Spingarn's throat, white teeth drawn apart.

Spingarn looked, evaded the rush, and twisted Marvell into a spitting heap, mouth full of sand.

"The loon!" bawled Hawk, raising his musket. "Shall I shoot the deserter, Captain?"

Spingarn shook his head. Marvell looked up, astonished.

"What—" he said, wiping his mouth.

"Forget it," said Spingarn. "It's over."

Marvell looked down at his body. He saw that the paunch was gone. Memory came back.

"Spingarn! It's you!"

"Captain?" asked Hawk again. He indicated his musket.

"No, Sergeant," Spingarn said firmly. "It is truly over!"

"Sir?" asked Horace. "The Alien? I cannot record the unusual energy-fields now."

"Gone," said Spingarn.

Marvell was staring at Liz. She smiled shyly.

"Me—" Marvell began. "I— We—"

"They said we might," Liz agreed.

Marvell grinned at Spingarn.

"All that aggression! With teeth, too! You were lucky, Spingarn! Hell's teeth, what was I?"

"Tell him," Spingarn ordered Horace.

Sergeant Hawk glared at the place where the ruins of the Genekey had stood.

"Captain," he said, pointing to the sandy waste. "Did old Hawk have the right of it? Ye see, I'd a notion of utterly bombarding Hell Gates and giving the Devil a touch of Woolwich powder to remind him that good Christians are not to be trifled with. Was I right to mine the Devil?"

Spingarn patted Hawk on the shoulder.

"You had the right of it, Sergeant. And the Devil's gone to find another Pit."

Liz Hassell felt a new and shameful coyness in the presence of Marvell. Absurd but nonetheless real.

"It's gone," she told him. "You did it."

Marvell found standing upright unfamiliar. He had an impulse to round his shoulders and allow his hands to touch the ground. He resisted it.

"I wouldn't have been able to help without you," he said.

Spingarn began to laugh.

A modest Marvell!

Marvell joined the laughter.

It was Hawk who broke the mood.

" 'Ware the Devil," he warned Spingarn. "That one is like the Frogs—he comes back when he's least expected."

Spingarn looked upward, to the blue-violet sky. Where had it gone, that eerie being? A cold echo of its frustrated glittering intelligence rang in his mind. *Was it truly gone from Talisker?*

CHAPTER

★ 17 ★

Getting Talisker's thousands of Time-outers back to Center proved a tiresome business. Spingarn turned them over to Horace. Blank, bored, shocked, bewildered, they were dimly aware that they had existed in strange territories. There were many casualties, of course. But their numbers had been increased by the normal process of reproduction. There were hundreds of child refugees from Hell.

The Alien's Possibility Space had maximized fecundity.

Liz Hassell found herself pregnant. Marvell was freshly astonished at his powers. His modesty wilted and faded, though his girth did not increase. He discovered that fitness was an invigorating condition: for several weeks after the retreat of the Alien, he and Liz rambled over Talisker's Frames, or such of them as had survived the collapse of the barriers. Together they plotted a dozen new variations on the new Frame that was to be established around the legend of Spingarn, the Probability Man. It was a time of pleasurable excitement for them both.

Marvell was only faintly disturbed to hear that Dyson had interfered with the Mechanical Age warfare scheme; it seemed that the elegant young Dyson had lowered the survival rate so much that the Plot was almost insatiable. There was actually a shortage of genuine suicidal psychopaths throughout the vast fabric of the Frames. Marvell sent a message suggesting that Dyson be recruited, but a bleak answer came back to say that he was already programmed into an almost forgotten Frame that projected the end of life on Terra, a Frame of long-headed crawling men and women with no relief from eternal bitter rain. Liz felt sorry for the slim Dyson, but only briefly. Her main interest was in the process of reproduction. In Ethel, she found a garrulous soul-mate.

Spingarn gradually learned the minimal importance of the male in society. Now that her future was assured, and that of the twins, Ethel had no time to discuss the implications of all they had been through together. That they had lived as elemental beasts, that they had together endured the fantastic whims of the Alien in Talisker's crazy Frames, meant nothing to her: here, now, the twins. That was her cosmos.

When the directive came, Spingarn was almost glad.

Talisker would revert to its museum status.

It was the end of a vast, cosmic experiment. The Alien had crawled out of the underground pit in which it had lain for a hundred million years, and now it was gone to build an approximation of its own environment.

And Spingarn?

Spingarn endured Marvell's banal excitement during the relatively slow journey back to Center. No tricks of warping away the eerie dimensions this time in the latest vessels. Talisker was no longer a priority. Sergeant Hawk was glumly aware of his captain's increasing state of depression. He tried to cheer him up daily, with accounts of this or that half-mythical encounter with the ghastly things that had once been the victims of random cell-fusion; the sergeant's career had reached a splendid climax, for he was convinced that he had been instrumental in destroying a dangerous alliance between the tribes of the French and the Devil; he was careful to glorify Spingarn's part, however.

Not all his martial boasting could counter Spingarn's miserable sense of anticlimax. Constantly his thoughts returned to the strange intelligence he had liberated. He could recall the vast and hopeless hunger for identification that had possessed the disinterred Alien: it had come from the deep rocks with a problem of personal identification that no human mind could conceive of. And it was gone from Talisker.

Only the empty ruins were left.

The black eyes glistened like damp pebbles. Spingarn had made his report, produced his recommendations, and announced his plans.

"You expect congratulations, Spingarn?" the Director asked. *"You!"*

Spingarn could still trace the features of the frightful thing the Director had once been. That terrible transmutation, now reversed, had been a red-lipped rearing snake-headed beast that had fed on living things brought by its robot attendants; for years it had lived in the fetid, stinking mud of the low cavern at the center of the web of structures at Frames Control. For years, the man who now stared with undying hate in his eyes at the returning Spingarn had suffered from the effects of Spingarn's experiments with random despecialized cell transforms.

Even now the man was snake-like. The attenuated neck, the flat black eyes, the hiss of indrawn breath: all were most terribly a reminder of that lunging and ferocious beast that the Director had become. Spingarn knew there was no forgiveness.

"I don't expect anything," Spingarn said. "I did what you asked. I completed the instructions given me by the Guardians."

Marvell was there too. So was Liz Hassell. Deneb watched impassively, though there was a cautious regard for Spingarn in his eyes. A man of action, he recognized the strange, compelling aura of vitality in Spingarn's short, wide-shouldered frame.

"They all did their assigned duty," Deneb pointed out. "Comp initially gave us a low reading on the probability of success, sir. Statistically, one or more of them should have succumbed in the Alien Possibility Space. Survival of all three was most exceptional in the math we have."

Marvell was almost his ebullient self again.

"It is over!" he exclaimed. "Christ, we did it! I gave the Alien a viewpoint it could recognize—me, Marvell! There isn't any Alien interference in Talisker—all that Uncertainty Factor you were getting in the Frames is out!"

Spingarn could barely realize that it was over, as Marvell said. Star systems had grown, bloomed and died during the time the Alien had endured on Talisker. And now that vast and almost impenetrable being had flown into some cosmic hideaway to determine its own nature. *Gone!*

And with it the function of Spingarn in the Frames of Talisker!

It had taken weeks for Spingarn to realize that his special identity was gone.

He was no longer—no longer!—the Probability Man!

The Director glared at Marvell and questioned him and Liz Hassell about the fantastic encounter between the transmuted Marvell, Liz, Spingarn and the Alien. Liz was brief and coherent, Marvell spluttered repetitiously, the Director examining them with that combination of icy intelligence and hateful irony that was his chief characteristic.

Spingarn smiled as Marvell told of his plans to build an entire Frame around the exploits of Spingarn the Probability Man. He could retire. No more grotesque encounters, no more violence. A peaceful, humdrum existence in some minor capacity in Frames Control. The twins clearly needed a firm hand: Spingarn would supply it.

"We're sure the Alien's gone," said Liz. "We got readings of power losses from all over the Galaxy which corresponded with the release of some kind of extra-universal energy-field—Comp checked them out, and it's sure there's an unparalleled surge."

Spingarn could imagine it.

All through the Galaxy, the Alien would have reached out to gather in the tendrils of its presence. It would have interfered, in its bizarre way, with the gravitational systems of a billion stars. Tremors of shockwaves had been recorded clear across the vast reaches of the arms of the island-universe as the Alien gathered itself together for a leap into *otherness*.

"You think it's over, Spingarn?" snarled the Director, seeing his abstraction. "Is it?"

"Yes," said Spingarn. "It's over."

Deneb said tiredly: "Most of the Uncertainty Factors are gone. We can clear up the rest."

"Miss Hassell?" the Director asked. "You showed an excellent appreciation of Talisker once before. Do you say it's over?"

Spingarn held his breath. There was more than evil malice in the terrible old man's intent face.

Liz smiled nervously. She had heard enough of Talisker, Alien, Spingarn, Probability Theory and the effects of random cell-fusion.

"It's over," she said. "Yes."

"Marvell?" asked the Director.

"Yes! We go ahead with the Frame—all of it! There'll be Spingarn Frames for generations—no end to them!"

"Spingarn?"

"I think so," said Spingarn unsurely.

Was there something he had missed?

"Take him to the Guardians," the Director said.

"And Miss Hassell and Marvell?" Deneb asked.

The Director shrugged. They were nothing to him.

"Reinstated."

Liz whispered that she was resigning, but the Director had no interest. She left the low blue-pulsing room wondering what would become of Spingarn.

Marvell said wistfully: "I wish there was some record of us, Liz! How about ape-men? But we could never do the body structuring—not *real,* I mean."

Liz smiled tolerantly.

"That Alien helping me! Look what it did with Spingarn—imagine Marvell and the Alien in Plotting! What a combination!"

"I think I'll go to see Ethel," said Liz.

There were important matters to discuss.

"Captain!" roared Hawk as they reached the inner recesses of Frames Control. "Look where the poxy dogs have brought me—loon-faced clockwork monkeys!"

Deneb had gone, and Spingarn was before the robots who called themselves the Guardians. Squat and impressive, they had more authority than any human. All the long years of the accumulation of knowledge and understanding were at their steely fingertips. *Why had the evil Director sent him into this robotic sanctuary?*

The robots raised steel claws in salute.

"Four of 'em!" Hawk spat disgustedly. "And 'Orris babbling like a maniac out there! What's an old soldier to make of it, eh, Captain?"

"I don't know either, Sergeant."

There was a strangely pitying look in the metal faces.

"You were almost successful, Spingarn!" one of the Guardians announced.

Almost ...

Spingarn sensed again some factor he could not calculate swimming below the level of his consciousness. Mazes of uncertainties and the higher math of Probability Curves danced through his consciousness. A sense of purpose was there too.

"It's gone," Spingarn said firmly. "Gone."

"According to our readings, yes," the second Guardian said. "Almost certainly gone, at least for a longer time than is necessary for the human race to consider."

Spingarn felt the long aeons of time carving tunnels through the Alien's bizarre presence. When humans were no more, would it still live in its approximation of being?

"There are still certain anomalies, you see, Spingarn," the third robot suggested.

"Aye!" muttered Hawk. "More Frog talk! Bowels of God, Captain, ye have a strange acquaintance!"

"Wait, Sergeant," commanded Spingarn.

The first Guardian spoke again for all.

"The Head of Disaster Control mentioned certain areas where your own random procedures were operative."

The four metal figures waited.

Spingarn shivered. More of those blazing, weird adventures? But what of Ethel? The twins?

"Deneb said he could clear them."

"He was wrong," the fourth Guardian said. "You see, neither he nor his agents have your unique abilities."

"Or your experience," the first Guardian added.

"Knew the Devil of Devils wouldn't be put down so easily!" snorted Hawk. "Cunning boggarts!"

Spingarn relaxed. "Go on," he told the Guardians.

After all, he was the Probability Man.

Ethel was unsurprised when he told her of the instructions he had received. She smiled, assured him that she was well-provided for—which she was—and asked when he would return. Spingarn was quite sure she did not listen to his answer.

"I'm taking the sergeant," he said.

"What a good idea!"

"And Horace."

"Now that is sensible! I wonder if Liz can come over for a little farewell supper. I'll see!"

The black and white collie bitch wagged her tail and followed Ethel.

The ship was stained with the patina of galactic dust and cosmic radiance. Ethel brought the twins to see it shimmer, hover for a few seconds in an uncanny radiance as it held for a while an unreal balance between electromagnetic and gravitational forces, and then vanish in a blaze of fragmented molecules that still rang with the violence of imploding energies.

They blinked and stared solemnly. Ethel sighed.

"Daddy's gone!" she told them. "Gone to see if he can make another legend for you darlings to hear one day! Gone beyond the stars and through the dark!"

They laughed now.

"Gone to the Changed Worlds," she said softly. "I saw them with your daddy once. He'll come back and tell you what he did." She looked at the ringing space where the ship had stood. "He'll come back," she said to herself now. "He's a hard bastard. He'll have to be."

DAW sf
BOOKS